JACK CHRISTIE
ADVENTURES
DAY OF VENGEANCE

Praise for the Jack Christie Adventures

For Sally, Tom, Peter and Anna – J. O'B.

A TEMPLAR BOOK

First published in the UK in 2011 by Templar Publishing,
an imprint of The Templar Company Limited,
The Granary, North Street, Dorking,
Surrey, RH4 1DN, UK

www.templarco.co.uk

First edition

ISBN 978-1-84877-103-1

Cover design by www.the-parish.com

Eiffel tower artwork by Ian Andrew
Map design by Will Steele

Edited by Anne Finnis, Helen Greathead and Ruth Martin

Image credits: p.38 Hitler in Paris © CORBIS; p.85 Spitfires © Fox
Photos/Stringer/Hulton Archive/Getty Images; p.221 V-2 Rocket ©
Bettman/CORBIS; p. 253 Map of WW2 © Mary Evans / Retrograph Collection

Printed and bound by CPI Group (UK) Ltd, Croydon, CR0 4YY

JACK

ADVENTURES

CHRISTIE

DAY OF VENGEANCE

templar

The Year: 1940

The Place: Paris, occupied France

The Mission: To stop the Second World War going nuclear

In Jack Christie's third adventure, Jack and Angus travel back in time to the Second World War where they witness the Battle of Britain, occupied Paris and an attempted assassination of Adolf Hitler.

But can they stop a premature Nazi Vengeance programme and prevent the Second World War from going nuclear in Europe?

Contents

Jack's Adventures So Far...

It has been eight months since Jack and Angus discovered that their school, Soonhope High, is a front for a team of scientists who control the most powerful technology ever conceived: the technology of time travel. At the heart of this technology is a machine called the Taurus. Jack's father, Professor Tom Christie, led the team that originally designed it. But for a single fleeting encounter, Jack hasn't seen his father since he was six, when the scientists who formed the Taurus had a fatal disagreement and Christie was forced into exile, leaving Jack and his wife, Carole, behind in Soonhope in the Borders of Scotland. Christie's plan was to harness time travel to make changes to the past – like stopping wars so that today's world might become a better place. He attracted some passionate and brilliant supporters from the original team, including Dr Pendelshape who, until recently, was Jack's History teacher at Soonhope. Pendelshape and Christie – together with their small band of followers, who call themselves 'Revisionists' – have developed sophisticated computer simulations to model interventions in the past that can benefit mankind.

Their former colleagues, on the other hand, continue to believe that changing events in the past, however well meant, is dangerous and may have unforeseen consequences. Once Christie was out of the way, they formed a group called 'VIGIL' to ensure that the Taurus was kept secret, but in working order, should it ever be needed. They housed the Taurus in an underground complex beneath an old school on the Soonhope estate, which they later reopened to act as a front. The teachers have ordinary jobs at the school, but have second lives as members of VIGIL. They stand ready to use the Taurus, should it ever be needed.

Jack and Angus became embroiled when, unknown to VIGIL, Christie created a second Taurus and proceeded to try to stop the event that triggered the First World War – the assassination of the Archduke Ferdinand, in Sarajevo in June, 1914. Pendelshape acted as Christie's partner, continuing to teach at Soonhope and leading VIGIL to believe that he was loyal to them. Meanwhile, Jack and Angus were used as pawns in a battle between the two camps. Jack's loyalties were torn. In the end, having witnessed at first hand the dangers of time travel and intervening in the past, Jack decided that the right course of action was to side with VIGIL. Not knowing the whereabouts of Christie's base, VIGIL can do nothing about the second Taurus. Christie, on the other hand, will not use his Taurus while Jack is under the guard of VIGIL, for fear VIGIL members might take retribution on his son.

But soon after the failed attempt to intervene in the assassination in Sarajevo, Pendelshape hatched a new plan to intervene in time – this time in Elizabethan England. Pendelshape and the Revisionist team were excited about these new plans, but became frustrated when Christie refused to take part in them, again concerned about the consequences for Jack. Christie became isolated from the Revisionists and finally decided to leave, concerned for his own safety. Knowing that Pendelshape and his former friends would press on with the new plan, Christie took the unprecedented step of warning VIGIL and Jack of this new attempt to intervene in the past. Jack and Angus found themselves once again caught up in VIGIL's plans to thwart the Revisionists. In the end they succeeded. But the location of the Revisionists' base and Taurus are still unknown to VIGIL and Jack's father remains a fugitive. Although the architect of the Taurus, he finds himself cast out both by his former colleagues in VIGIL and now by the Revisionists. Meanwhile, Pendelshape is thought to have died, but his body was never found…

Gottschalk Farm

Germany – March 1918

It was Axel's favourite game. Mother had finally released him from his early morning chores on the farm and he raced across the garden into the narrow strip of woodland that separated their place from the Stockel's next door. The woods held a secret. At least it was a secret to Axel and his friend Hans. A little stream dipped and darted its way through the undergrowth of the woods – a miniature assault course of gurgling rapids and twinkling pools criss-crossed by fallen branches from the old trees above. He had shown it to Hans, who often came up from the village to play, and they once tried to find the source of the stream, up in the low rolling hills above Kulsheim, until they had got stuck in a muddy bog. Mother had not been happy when they got back late and dirty. Today, Axel wasn't going to wait for Hans. Spring was arriving, but there was still a bite in the air and there had been a downpour the night before, which meant that the stream would be swollen with water. Perfect.

Axel prized his way through the hole in the fence and pushed on up to the starting point, where the stream rounded the gnarled roots of an old oak tree. He opened his bag and carefully removed its precious contents. He held the object up with both hands, so that it caught the morning sunlight that filtered through the branches above. A model battleship. Even at ten years old,

Axel was an expert on all the big ships of the German High Seas Fleet. He could remember the big excitement after their victory at Jutland over the British. That had been two years ago, and now, although he sometimes found it difficult to follow what Mother and Father said, he knew that the war was nearly over. General Ludendorff had launched a huge attack in the west and the talk was that Germany would soon win the war. The gossip in the village was that the prison camp to the north might soon be expecting another wave of prisoners from the front line.

Father was very excited. The shortages would be over and Germany would be victorious. Father had volunteered right at the start of the war and there was a picture of Axel standing next to him in his uniform, with some of the others from the village, before they went off to fight. After he had been away for a while, the atmosphere in the house changed. Mother seemed tired and anxious. Then they got the news. Father was in hospital – he had been injured and had to be operated on. He lost his lower leg. But, of course, it could have been much worse. Axel remembered the day he returned. Everyone was excited. His father was a hero; Axel was very proud. But when he arrived home, Axel was disappointed. His father did not really turn out to be the great man of Axel's memory and imagination. There was the injury of course. He could walk OK, but he limped and needed a stick and this made him stoop. But what bothered Axel most was that he did not talk very much and, when Axel looked into his eyes, it was if there was no one there. His father was strangely distant and Axel didn't really know why.

Axel inspected the battleship. Father had helped him build it originally, but Axel had made a number of important modifications since its last voyage. He was convinced that it would now be a winner. After much consideration, he had even given the ship a name. SMS *König*, after a Kaiser Class battleship that had taken part in the battle at Jutland. It had ten twelve-inch main battle guns. To anyone else, the ship may have appeared little more than a series of crude wooden blocks and matchsticks. But in Axel's mind his own *König* was more than worthy of the German High Seas Fleet. Now it was about to undergo sea trials and Axel was convinced that his ship would have the edge on Hans's ship, when they next raced them down the stream.

With precision, Axel cupped the hull of the boat and leaned down to the bubbling stream. He allowed the bow to nose the water, where it eddied into a small pool away from the main current, and then *König* was launched. The boat glided forward, gently at first, but suddenly the current grabbed it and it was off. Axel could scarcely keep up as the boat bobbed and weaved its way down the swollen stream, crashing over the miniature waterfalls, sometimes disappearing from sight completely as the stream became lost under moss, heavy branches and vegetation which grew over the banks on either side. As the boat descended, faster and faster, Axel followed, racing down through the woodland, sometimes jumping from one bank to the other to get the best view. In a few minutes, the stream would enter the thicket at the bottom of the woods. From there it would exit into the fields beyond. Axel needed to be ready to pluck it from the water before it escaped into the field and then sailed bravely on, maybe to the Rhine and then possibly further into the North Sea itself.

Luckily, there was a small pool just before the thicket at the bottom of the wood, which temporarily slowed the boat's progress. This was the effective finishing point for all their races and gave ample opportunity for the boat to be rescued. Axel got there, pink and out of breath, just as *König* arrived, triumphant (and surprisingly, upright), with a little splash into the pool. In a manoeuvre which he had executed many times before, Axel leaped from one side of the pool to the other, whilst deftly reaching down and plucking the proud vessel from the water. On this occasion, as Axel's foot planted itself on the opposite bank, he slipped on the damp undergrowth and both he and the boat went flying. As Axel felt himself tumbling downwards out of control, oddly, the only thing that flashed through his mind was the fate of *König*. A second later he crashed head first into a thicket, where he came to rest, scratched and dazed.

Axel blinked and looked up.

He was not alone.

Before he could react, a large, dirty hand clamped over his mouth. Axel felt a wave of fear pulse through his body. A man was leaning over him, very close, and was peering into his eyes. The man was thin, dirty and dishevelled. He had hunted eyes that flicked back and forth nervously. His clothes were tatty and wet, but even though Axel was suddenly very scared, he registered that the clothes the man wore may at one time have been a military uniform. With a feeling of dread, Axel realised that he must be an escapee from the prisoner of war camp.

The man leaned close to Axel, put a grubby index finger to his lips and hissed, "Ssshhh."

He paused, breathing heavily. It was as if he was weighing something up in his mind. Suddenly, he hauled Axel to his feet and, keeping hold of the boy, pushed him back through the thicket. Instinctively Axel tried to wriggle free, but despite his emaciated state, the man was far too strong for him and Axel felt himself being bundled forward. From the corner of his eye, Axel caught sight of his boat in the undergrowth. He gave a little squeal as the man clumsily drove *König* into the ground with his boot as they pressed forward. The man stopped at the edge of the woods and looked up towards the farmhouse. All was quiet. With a grunt, he forced Axel over the fence and frogmarched him to the back door of the farm.

They entered the porch and then crashed through into the kitchen beyond. Axel's mother wheeled round in fright. She took one look at Axel and the strange dishevelled man, and screamed. It was a mistake. It seemed to make the man even more panicky and he suddenly took out a large black pistol from his trousers and pointed it at Axel's mother. She stepped back, held her hands to her face and started to sob uncontrollably.

The man spoke in a language that Axel did not understand, but he could tell that the man was scared. "Please. You must be quiet," he told them.

Axel's mother was shaking in fear. *"Mein Gott, mein Gott…"* she said, over and over again.

The man pointed to his mouth. "I am sorry for this. I need food, water and clothing. Then I will go. Do you understand?"

But neither Axel nor his mother did understand and his mother was too panic-stricken to respond. The man was becoming more and more agitated. He knew that he was running out of time.

"Please, give me what I want, and I will go. Food and water. No harm will come of you."

Suddenly, Axel heard the front door open and then the distinctive knock of his father's wooden leg on the floorboards. He heard his father's voice call out, *"Ich hörte das Schreien."* And then, a little more urgently, *"Maria – was ist los?"*

Axel could clearly hear his father's footsteps approaching. He saw his mother's eyes dart to the door. Suddenly, the door swung open. Axel's father stood there, a look of horror on his face. He raised his stick. The man panicked, swung the gun round and fired a single shot. Axel's father slumped to the floor. His mother screamed. For a moment, the man stood there... and then, he ran.

Axel's mother knelt over her husband, pawing at his shirt, crying and screaming. It had happened so quickly and for a moment Axel did not understand. The body of his father, the great war hero, lay sprawled awkwardly across the floor of the kitchen. His eyes stared lifelessly at the ceiling and a trickle of blood oozed from one corner of his mouth. At first, Axel did not cry and did not feel any emotion. It was as if the violence of the act was too much for one so young to understand.

Trancelike, Axel walked from the kitchen, through the back porch and down into the garden. It was only then that he started to run. He ran faster and faster, until he reached the wood and the little stream. He ran down the stream, the trees flashing past him on either side. As he ran, tears gathered in the corners of his eyes. The faster he ran, the more he cried. Finally, he stopped at the bottom of the woods next to the little pool. He jumped across the pool and there he saw it. Half buried in the mud and partially crushed lay the battleship *König*. He reached down, picked it up and held it tightly to his chest.

Their Finest Hour
Kent, England – August 1940

Then Jack spotted it. A single BF109 heading for home. "This is Red Two. Snapper ten o'clock low. Tally-Ho! Tally-Ho!"

"Good luck Red Two."

"Breaking – port forty-five degrees."

Jack tipped the Supermarine Mark 1B into a steep dive. The twenty-seven litre Merlin III engine screamed as the Spitfire topped four hundred miles an hour, slicing through the freezing air. As Jack levelled out, the G-force crushed him into his seat. Surely the wings would be ripped from the fuselage? But he had managed it perfectly. He peered through the spinning disc of the airscrew at the yellow-nosed Messerschmitt 109 only a hundred metres ahead. The German pilot hadn't noticed Jack on his tail, so focused was he on his run for the Channel. Jack flicked the gun button to fire and put the reflector sight on. He eased the dot in the middle onto the 109's fuselage and, as he eased closer, the Messerschmitt drew into the cross hairs. Jack pressed the button. The four .303 Browning machine guns and the two 20mm Hispano canons let rip and the cockpit filled with the smell of cordite. The flank of the 109 was peppered. Instantly, glycol from the cooling system ignited and there was an explosion of white vapour. The 109 flipped onto its back and started to arc into a long, lazy dive. A few seconds before, the German pilot had been heading for home – free. Now he was dead and plummeting to an icy grave, still strapped to his seat. Jack was hypnotised and trailed the 109 towards the metallic grey of the sea, far below.

It was a schoolboy error.

The first Jack knew about it was from the streak of angry tracer that missed his perspex canopy by millimetres. A second 109. He should have known better. They always hunt in pairs.

"Red One, Red One – Snapper on my tail."

But the R/T just crackled. Red One wasn't coming to his rescue any time soon.

He remembered Angus's words to him not an hour before: "Never fly straight and level for more than twenty seconds. If you do, you'll die."

The Supermarine Spitfire and the Messerschmitt BF109 were the best fighter planes of their day. They were comparable but each had particular strengths. Jack's training cut in as he remembered the one strength of the Spitfire, which might just save his life. He threw the Spit into a savage turn and glanced over his shoulder. The 109 was still with him – a dirty orange flash from its guns showed that the German was still clamped to his tail like a limpet. Jack heard rounds rip into his fuselage and suddenly a bullet passed right through his canopy, millimetres from his face. Jack cursed his luck. Trust him to pick a fight with a real pro. He gulped in oxygen from the clammy mask.

Jack tightened the turn and glanced at the instruments to see how badly he was hit – glycol at 100 degrees; oil pressure 70lbs – miraculously still OK – but suddenly his head felt heavy...

the brutal speed and tightness of the turn was causing him to black out. If he could hold on he might just survive. Words from his training flashed through his head, *"A Spit can turn tighter than a 109 – hold it long enough and the 109 can't stay with you – he will trace a gradually widening circle in the sky and you may just live…"*

Suddenly, the Spitfire started to shake – a high-speed stall. Jack bit his lip to stop himself losing consciousness and a drop of blood trickled down the inside of his mask. He knew it was possible to hold the Spit in the stall… *if* you were a good enough pilot. He was about to find out if he was. Jack made a second turn and snatched a glance at the pursuing 109. Suddenly he saw it wobble – it was also stalling – Jack's heart soared… the German pilot was being forced to ease the turn to avoid engine failure. It was a matter of millimetres but it would save Jack's life. A few more mad loops in the sky and Jack started to gain on the 109. His neck muscles were screaming for him to stop, but in seconds the tables would be turned and Jack would have the 109 in his own cross hairs. Sure enough the 109 crept into his sight. Jack felt the adrenaline surge through him and he stabbed the fire button. Again, he heard the staccato rip of his guns, but he had fired prematurely and the rounds flew high and wide. He tried again. Nothing. He was out of ammo already.

Abruptly, his adversary released the 109 from its turn and, just for a moment, Jack caught his eyes peeking out from the white strip of face between helmet and mask. The German pilot touched his temple briefly with an outstretched palm – it was a wry acknowledgement, which meant simply, "Until next time, my friend."

The sun flashed briefly on the grey tail fin of the 109 as he finally broke for home and then... he was gone.

Jack was alone again in the great blue emptiness, ten thousand feet above the green meadows of Kent.

Alive.

The Project

Angus thumped Jack on the back, "Great dogfight. He nearly had you. What do you think?"

"Love it – very realistic," Jack replied.

"Yeah, these guys also make proper flight simulation kits, you know, for training pilots. I've used it on my pilot's course," Angus said.

Jack paused the simulation session and put down the joystick.

"How's that going?"

"I'm up to forty hours now. We were up at the airstrip yesterday near Edinburgh."

"But no Spitfires, eh?"

"Well, there is one up there – owned by some enthusiast. But he's the only one daft enough to fly it – it's nearly seventy years old after all. Would you fly a plane that old?"

Jack nodded at the console, "Wouldn't mind if it's anything like that."

"Mind you, Dad says he's talked to the guy who owns it – apparently it's still great to fly – even after all those years. Anyway, if you wait long enough, you might have a chance..." Angus grinned.

"What do you mean?"

"Come on, I'll show you – you're going to love this."

Angus bolted from his bedroom at the top of the old farmhouse and Jack followed as he tumbled down the stairs which creaked under his weight. They passed the living room where Angus's dad had his feet up on a stool, puffing a pipe, reading *Soonhope News*.

"Dad – I'm just showing Jack, you know, your *project*…"

Mr Jud put down the paper as they hurried passed. "OK, but don't touch anything… might join you in a sec…"

They crossed the courtyard of the farm and made their way down to one of the old barns. It was a beautiful June day. The Jud's farm looked idyllic next to the wood-fringed pond, surrounded by the low rolling hills of the Border country.

Angus heaved open the large barn door, "Here…"

He switched on a light and Jack adjusted his eyes to the gloom. There were some large sheets of metal scattered about, bits of engineering equipment and some sort of enormous engine suspended by two chain hoists hanging from the roof.

Angus spread out his arms like a magician, "Ta-da!"

"What is it?" Jack asked.

"Isn't it obvious?"

Then Jack saw it. To the rear of the old barn resting on a series of wooden trestles was what looked like the fuselage of an aeroplane. There was only one problem – it didn't have any wings.

"A plane. That's your dad's 'project'?"

Mr Jud came into the barn, sliding the door open a bit wider. Sunlight flooded in.

"Not just any old project Jack, and not just any old plane."

He spoke in a rumbling voice with a strong Scottish accent. He had the same powerful build as Angus, but his face was leathered and creased from years working the sheep farm.

Jack looked at Mr Jud. "No?"

Mr Jud marched over to the fuselage and patted it firmly on the flank, as if it was a prize cow he was fattening up for market.

"She's a legend."

Angus couldn't hold back any longer. "A genuine Battle of Britain Spitfire!"

"A Mark One B," Mr Jud added, a note of reverence in his voice.

"Incredible." Jack stared in wonder at the old plane. "You're restoring it?"

Angus laughed, "Trying to… a bit of a labour of love, eh Dad?"

Mr Jud shrugged. "That's right, son – it'll take years… but one day…" Mr Jud looked up at the ceiling of the barn as if he was having some sort of religious experience, "one day she will fly and we shall touch the face of God…"

Angus looked at his feet self-consciously. "Er, right Dad."

"Where are the wings?" Jack asked, trying to bring him back down to earth.

"Well there's the story, Jack. An incredible story really." Mr Jud ushered them over to a cork message board on one side of the barn, which had all sorts of old photos and diagrams stuck to it. He pulled down one of the pictures.

"See that?"

Jack squinted at the old black-and-white photo.

"The Eiffel Tower. In Paris?"

"Yes. But look again – what do you see there…?" Mr Jud stabbed a thick dirty fingernail at the top of the photo, "…towards the top section of the tower?"

Jack narrowed his eyes. He didn't see it at first, the picture seemed to have been taken on quite a misty day, but then, yes, he was sure of it – there was the tail fin of an aeroplane sticking out of the tower. Somehow the main fuselage must have been buried inside the metal latticework of the great Paris landmark, but the tail fin was still hanging out.

"You're not telling me…"

Mr Jud laughed. "Aye, Jack… and this was the very plane. *The very plane.*"

"Unbelievable. What happened?"

"There was a German air raid on Northolt, which is now near Heathrow Airport, near London. It was in June, during the early part of the Second World War, just before the Battle of Britain started properly. This Spitfire was scrambled and got into a rare old dogfight. Later, apparently, it pursued the attackers out over the Channel, but got caught in cloud. Very disorientating. The Spit made it all the way to Paris but couldn't put down for some reason. Anyway, it flew straight into the Eiffel Tower!"

"The pilot died obviously?"

"Actually, no one knows who he was. He was never found. It is possible that he bailed out before the crash. It's one of the strangest things about the story."

"I suppose that explains the wings."

"Aye. The wings were both ripped from the fuselage as the plane flew into the tower. Presumably because there was no fuel left, or very little, there was no fire. Shortly after the photo was taken the whole thing dislodged itself from the tower in the wind and it fell to the ground. After the war, they found it in bits in some warehouse and it was transported back to the UK. It was a gift from the French to the British."

"And you have it here now?"

"Cost me a bob or two – but yes, there she is. It's taken me this long to assemble her even to this stage."

"And that's not all, is it Dad?" Angus said, enthusiastically. "Tell him."

"Well, Jack, you know about my grandfather, Ludwig?"

Jack gave a furtive glance at Angus, "Oh yes, Mr Jud, Angus has told me all about him."

"Well, as you know, he was a German soldier. He fought in the First World War. But he was injured and captured by the British and ended up in a British hospital. There he met Dot, my grandmother. She was a nurse in the field hospital. She was Scottish. The war ended. They got married and he never went home. Eventually he moved here and took over the farm. He became a British citizen. He liked the Brits – thought we were an eccentric lot. He was funny – I remember when I was a kid, he'd do a great impression of an English upper-class toff."

Angus interrupted, "He fought in the Second World War as well, but on the *British side*. Amazing, eh?"

"He was interested in machines of all sorts – bit of a family tradition, as you know," Mr Jud continued. "He got into flying, joined an amateur club and the RAF before the war. He was posted up here, but as the war got closer he was reassigned to the south-east. They had to rent out the farm – good pilots were scarce and very valuable."

"That's amazing."

"If you come back up to the house, we'll show you some of his old stuff. Come on."

Mr Jud and Angus turned and walked back out into the sunshine.

For a moment, Jack lingered in the musty barn, surrounded by the metal detritus of the rusty old fighter plane. Jack didn't know a lot about the history but he knew enough. Seventy years before, this little plane and others like it, piloted by a few hundred airmen, had swooped and soared over the gentle countryside of south-east England in a grim battle for survival as Britain stood alone against the Nazi war machine.

Jack slid his outstretched palm across the smooth metal of the fuselage and with his fingers he traced the outline of the red-and-blue concentric circles of the RAF roundel. It was worn, but still visible. He touched the ragged, rusted outline of the breach in the fuselage, where the port wing had been ripped free in the crash into the tower. He peered through the crack in the side into the bottom of the cockpit and he could make out the seat, dials and controls. He noticed that on the side of the cockpit and on the seat and in the foot well there was curious brown staining. Jack's heart gave a little jump when he realised that it was probably dried blood from the pilot as he was injured on impact.

"You coming or what?" Angus stuck his head around the barn door, "You've got to see this stuff of Dad's. It's so cool. Come on!"

Jack followed Angus back up to the farmhouse. In the living room Mr Jud had opened up an old wooden box and distributed its contents all over the floor. There were lots of old black-and-white photos: pictures of airmen in uniform, aerodromes, Spitfires and Hurricanes taking off or being prepared, pilots playing cards and even some blurred pictures of aerial combat.

"Look at that one. Some fighter planes had cameras in them that were triggered when the guns were firing. That's a German Heinkel bomber being clobbered," Mr Jud said – possibly with a little more enthusiasm than was necessary.

"So your great grandfather Ludwig – he was allowed in the RAF? Even though he was German, you know, by birth?"

"Oh, he gained British nationality, remember, after the First World War, when he married Dot. I know it sounds a bit strange. But he kind of renounced his past and became a Brit. Eventually he made it to Flight Commander."

"But wasn't he too old to fight by the Second World War?"

"You're right that most of the pilots were very young – eighteen or nineteen even. But they were desperate for qualified pilots so Ludwig ended up doing his fair share of operational stuff. Like the Northolt Raid I was talking about."

"Yeah – what *was* that?"

"A bit of a wake-up call for the RAF for sure. The RAF's communications usually gave them a big advantage – radar gave warning of incoming aircraft and fighters could be scrambled into the air to meet them. But this time it broke down. They think it was some sort of intelligence leak. They did find out about a German spy ring at that time that may have had something to do with it. Something about scientific secrets. A number of aircraft were destroyed on the ground and pilots killed. But old Ludwig didn't hesitate, he jumped into a waiting Hurricane and got it into the air. Shot down a number of enemy aircraft that day – won a medal…"

Mr Jud pulled a shiny metal cross from the box, "...there you go – Distinguished Flying Cross. Don't know why I have never put it up on the mantelpiece." Mr Jud buffed the medal with the cuff of his old jumper and placed it next to the jar which still contained a piece of Ludwig's shin bone from his injury in the First World War.

"Why was it was all such a big deal – you know, the Battle of Britain?" Jack asked.

Mr Jud shrugged. "In some ways it wasn't. Actually only about five hundred allied pilots died during the four or so months of fighting, which in military terms was not very many. Compare that to the millions who died in some of the other campaigns, like on the Eastern front between the Soviet Union and Germany."

"And Britain won the Battle?"

"In so much as the Germans called off Operation Sea Lion, which was the plan to invade Britain after France had surrendered. In fact, just before the Battle of Britain, France had surrendered to Germany and quite a few people had lost hope. Winston Churchill was determined that Britain should fight on, alone or not."

Angus stared at one of the old photos, "So what happened?"

"The Germans launched air attacks from their new bases in France and the Netherlands. They needed to get control of the skies before any sea invasion could take place, but try as they might, the German Luftwaffe could not break down the RAF. Then, in return for British planes bombing Berlin, Hitler changed tactics to bomb British cities – this gave the RAF breathing space. Eventually, Hitler gave up and then in 1941 he turned his attention to the east – invading the Soviet Union. So the Battle of Britain kept Britain in the war and, because it could continue the fight this meant that later on, in 1944, the Allies were able to launch D-Day and reoccupy Western Europe. Without those pilots, Britain may have needed to agree a humiliating peace with the Nazis, or face invasion. The world would have ended up a very different place."

"Hey – what about this one?" Jack held up another photo.

Mr Jud took it from Jack and looked at it. "That one is quite famous too. It's a picture taken from a plane showing a V-2 rocket just as it is taking off from its launch site in northern France."

"I've heard of them too, you know, V-1s and V-2s…"

"Yes – the German Vengeance programme. Towards the end of the war, German scientists developed flying bombs, called V-1s – and then actual rockets, called V-2s, which they launched from sites in northern France, targeting London, Paris and the Netherlands. By that stage they were losing the war and Hitler was desperate to find a miracle weapon that could somehow tip the balance."

"But it didn't work?"

"No. For the time, the technology they developed was incredible. But it also drained resources from the production of more ordinary, but better tried and tested weapons. Although the V-1s and V-2s were very scary, they could not be produced in sufficient numbers to really have much of an impact."

"So the V-2 was like a proper rocket – like a missile?"

"Yes. In fact, after the war, the Americans and other countries recruited many of the best German scientists to help on their own weapons programmes. It was quite a scandal. Many worked on the Apollo space programme – you know that put people on the moon. The design of the moon rockets isn't so different from a V-2 – just a lot bigger."

"There are loads more newspaper cuttings and pictures here," Angus said, working his way through the box, "That's Hitler, isn't it?"

"Certainly is. He's standing in front of the Eiffel Tower in June 1940. The only time he visited Paris… I think you can see the old film footage of his visit on the Internet. Apparently, when that photo was taken, Hitler is supposed to have said to the photographer, 'Take one of me here, take the next one in front of Buckingham Palace and then the one after that in front of the skyscrapers in New York.'"

"What a nutter!" Angus said.

They were interrupted by Mrs Jud. "We'll have to go now, dear. Lads – there's some soup left over if you want it…"

"I nearly forgot…" Mr Jud said.

"What?"

"Mum and I, we're driving up to Edinburgh. We'll be gone over night."

"Oh yeah, the show, what is it again?"

"*The Sound of Music*, the son of one of Mum's friends is in it – Peter. He's playing Friedrich. They're touring all round the country," Mr Jud put his mouth behind his hand and whispered sarcastically, "Can't wait."

Mrs Jud shouted from the kitchen, "Are you ready, dear?"

Mr Jud was already up the stairs. "I'll meet you at the car."

Mrs Jud popped her head round the door. "Where is he?"

"He's just coming, Mum."

Adolf Hitler, accompanied by his chief architect Albert Speer (left) and sculptor Arno Breker, near the Eiffel Tower. Hitler reportedly said to his photographer, Heinrich Hoffmann, "Take this one, Hoffmann; then the next one in Buckingham Palace and the next in front of the skyscrapers."

"So you two will be OK?"

"Yes, Mum."

"There is more in the fridge and that's Mark's number if you need any help with the animals. You're sure you'll be OK?"

"Yes, Mum. Go. Have fun."

Mrs Jud checked her make-up in the hall mirror one final time and shouted up the stairs. "I'm going. Now!"

Finally, Mr and Mrs Jud left the house and a few minutes later the boys watched the old Subaru kicking up dust from its back wheels as it disappeared up the farm track to the main road.

Angus rubbed his hands. "OK – lunch. And then we can go and have another shot on the Flight Simulator…" Angus smiled mischievously. "Or we can always take the bikes out…"

"I'll give that one a miss, thanks."

Soon they were sitting around the big wooden farm table digging into the soup.

"I'm going to sort out some toast. Want some?"

"OK," Jack said. "So how long do you think it will take to restore the plane?"

"Maybe it can't be done – you know, finding or remaking some of the parts… There's a lot missing. It's really expensive. To be honest, I think Dad might have overdone it this time."

"So you reckon you'll have your private pilot's licence before then?"

"For sure. I've only another few training hours to go. Paying for it is another matter, though."

"I'm sure VIGIL will loan you some cash, you know, for services rendered," Jack said, smiling.

Angus looked up and waved his spoon in the air. "You know what, that is a VERY good idea. We *should* be paid. After all, VIGIL can't possibly have any problem with cash…"

"No problem at all… if they get a bit short, they can just time travel to the vaults of the Bank of England and pick up a gold bar or two…"

Angus gazed into space, contemplating the exciting possibilities that time travel might offer for financial remuneration. "Imagine that… sometimes I think our Revisionist friends might have the right idea…"

"Sadly, I don't think they're in it for money… they have other reasons… like changing the world."

Angus turned back from the toast, sat down and started to slurp his soup.

"That's gross by the way," Jack said.

"Efficient though. Mind you, I'll tell you something," Angus wiped his mouth. "I like how VIGIL keep coming up with cool stuff…"

"They haven't got a choice… the Revisionists are still out there… they never found Pendelshape. In theory they could strike again. VIGIL need to keep on their toes; keep innovating."

"Right." Angus did not seem interested in Jack's point. "Like, have you checked out the new iPhone thing they've dished out to us all?" Angus pulled an iPhone from his pocket and started to slide his finger around on the screen. "So it looks like a normal iPhone and it's a mobile with apps and stuff, but then you put in the special code and it turns all VIGIL and you can access all these cool VIGIL apps…"

Jack rolled his eyes, "Yes – I was in the same training session… and remember, it's not just for cool apps, it's for VIGIL to keep an eye on us – security, tracking where we are – and for access to the history archives. It has an amazing amount of detail – even technical stuff on inventions…" Jack pulled out his own VIGIL iPhone. "See – here's mine…"

"Oh God – the toast!" Angus exclaimed.

Smoke billowed from the toaster by the window. Angus raced over to mount a rescue attempt… but all that was left were two lumps of charcoal.

"Great."

"Hello, what's this?"

Jack was peering at his iPhone screen. "I've got a message."

"First time for everything, Jack."

"Funny. Probably Mum hassling me."

Jack tapped the screen.

But it wasn't his mum and Jack's heart missed a beat when he read the message:

```
JACK - GET TO SAFETY. VIGIL IS ABOUT TO BE
ATTACKED. AM ALSO WARNING VIGIL COMMAND.
                    DAD.
```

Big Air

Jack nudged Angus and flashed the text in front of him. The colour drained from Angus's face. Jack looked up from the iPhone and it was right at that point that he noticed something strange in the smoky kitchen air. A thin beam of red light traced a line from the window to the wall at the back of the kitchen. It was only visible where it caught the smoke in the air. Jack's eye followed the beam of light to where it formed a tiny red dot which danced on the wall opposite.

"Look. What's…?"

But Angus had already grabbed him and was manhandling him to the floor. "Down!"

Jack and Angus hit the ground just as the first round from the sniper rifle shattered the kitchen window and embedded itself in the wall opposite.

"Someone's *shooting* at us from the woods…"

"I've got another message."

EMERGENCY MESSAGE FROM VIGIL: CODE RED. ALL VIGIL PERSONNEL TO ADOPT EMERGENCY PROTOCOL AND REPORT TO VIGIL COMMAND. REMOTE SECURITY DETAILS MAY HAVE BEEN COMPROMISED.

Angus held up his phone.

"I've got the same one. We might be without security…"

"That means trouble."

Suddenly, a second piece of mortar dislodged from the wall. They hadn't even heard the shot.

"It's coming from over there. Maybe if we can go out through the side door… to the outhouses."

"But maybe there are others, maybe they have us surrounded."

"Well we can't just wait here for them to come and get us. If we can get to the outhouse, we have a chance. We keep the bikes there."

They raced from the kitchen and through the house to the side door. Angus pushed it ajar and sneaked a look.

"Can't see anything. Who are these guys?"

"Got to be some sort of Revisionist assault. They're taking a big risk."

"Why would they do that? Everyone knows VIGIL is impregnable."

"Maybe they're targeting VIGIL personnel. We have to get out of here. Look – the door to the outhouse is just over there. We can make it."

They burst from the door and sprinted to the outhouse. Shots rang out and plumes of dirt spat up from the ground. They tumbled through the outhouse door, sprawling onto the dusty floor beyond. The outhouse adjoined the garage which housed Mr Jud's Land Rover. Next to it were the bikes they used on the farm, including Angus's old two-stroke 125 Husqvarna. Next to this was his dad's big new KTM XC 450.

"We'll take the KTM – Dad will forgive me," Angus panted.

"We have to get to Soonhope and link up with VIGIL. God knows what's going on. There's no sign of our VIGIL security guys. Maybe they've been caught? If we stay here, we're toast," Jack said.

"I reckon they'll have the main track down to the road covered and the back way too." Angus mounted the KTM, fired the engine and twisted the throttle. The engine gave a low, torquey growl. "We'll have to go cross-country…"

Jack reluctantly clambered onto the back of the bike.

Angus half turned, "Ready?"

"No…"

"Hold tight, I'm not hanging around."

Without warning, the garage doors in front of them flew open. Two men stood there. They were carrying assault rifles.

Angus did not hesitate. He pulled in the clutch lever, kicked down to select first gear, and twisted the throttle. The engine wailed. But instead of aiming for the open garage door, he released the clutch, threw the bike round and the spinning back wheel spewed gravel and muck up into the eyes of the two men, who jumped back in surprise. The bike now pointed towards the back of the outhouse. A point of exit was not obvious. The bike shot forward and Jack shut his eyes, waiting for the impact with the rear wall. But Angus had other plans. They raced up a wooden ramp built into the wall on the inside of the building. It led to an upper floor – a sort of mezzanine level. It was surprisingly large and they slalomed through old hay bales and bits of rusting farm equipment. Jack opened his eyes. Then, when he realised what was about to happen, he closed them again. Dead ahead there was a large open doorway built into the back wall – a large access hatch from the upper floor. Angus pointed the bike straight at it and two seconds later they were airborne. The bike, Angus and Jack flew from the second storey hatchway out into the open. Jack braced himself. The bike hit the ground with an almighty crunch; the front forks compressed fully and then recoiled violently as the bike bounced. Incredibly, they remained upright.

Angus yelled in exhilaration. He redlined the engine as they powered on towards the farm track that led up Goat Law. Jack snatched a look behind and nudged Angus.

"They're on to us – they've got quad bikes."

It looked like they had a clear run to the hill track. But suddenly another man emerged from the woods just ahead on their right. He stared straight at the bike bearing down on him and fumbled for his weapon. Angus dropped a gear and the front wheel of the bike popped into the air. Standing proud on the footrests, with Jack clinging desperately to his torso, Angus pulled an impressive wheelie straight at the man, who dived for cover. The front wheel touched down again, and they started to weave up the track to the crest of the hill. Jack looked behind again.

"They're still coming."

Two quad bikes were following them up the track in hot pursuit, plumes of dust spraying up from behind them.

"We'll have to head up to the old drove road and down over the Grey Mare's Tail," Angus shouted. "Five miles at most."

He gunned the KTM and it pounded upwards. They crested the hill in under a minute. They were already six hundred metres up and there was a light breeze. Beyond them, were only the endless rolling, bare hills of the Border country. Two parallel dry stone dykes, about fifty metres apart, marked the course of the old drove road. In times past it was used to drive sheep to market. It made a natural thoroughfare, like a giant heather and grass motorway that went directly over the hills and, more importantly, led directly to the uplands above the Soonhope High School estate – VIGIL HQ. The only trouble was, there was little cover on the hilltops and they would easily be spotted by the pursuing quad bikes.

They raced on and in only fifteen minutes they could see the village of Soonhope way below, its windows glinting in the midday sun. Jack turned. The quad bikes were still there – now only five hundred metres behind and closing. A rough track led down from the old drove road to Soonhope, hugging the steep-sided valley. Nearby was the Grey Mare's Tail – a series of cascades that drained a small loch that nestled between the summits of the surrounding hills. The waterfall's biggest drop was over thirty metres high and in winter it grew to an impressive torrent. Now, though, the water was low and the stream traced a silver thread down the granite outcrops of the hillside.

The track down from the old drove road followed the waterfall most of the way, giving the occasional hiker stunning views of Soonhope Valley below. At certain points, the track would contort into a series of steep hairpins, in order to regulate the descent. As they went down, Angus expertly worked his way up and down the gears to maximise speed and control. The KTM handled superbly, but it was no use, the pursing four-wheeled quad bikes had better grip and stability on the steep track and the distance between them was narrowing steadily.

Jack pummelled Angus on the back.

"They're closing… we've had it."

Angus pulled the bike up onto a rocky outcrop that overlooked a spectacular section of the waterfall. A crude wooden bench sat on top of the outcrop. It allowed Sunday walkers a chance to rest and enjoy the view. Directly in front of it, there was a dilapidated fence that, in theory anyway, prevented you from getting too close to the edge. Nearby, a sign gave thoughtful health and safety advice:

DANGER – CLIFF

To help those challenged with written English, there was a picture of a man tumbling upside down over the edge, surrounded by an avalanche of rocks. The man's survival looked to be in some doubt.

Although steep and craggy, the waterfall was only about ten metres across at this point. On the other side of the waterfall, but some way below the outcrop, the track re-appeared and crossed the stream over a narrow bridge.

Angus looked round. He powered the bike a few metres back up the track from where they had just come. As he revved the engine, the two quad bikes came round the last hairpin. Their pursuers had finally caught up. The quad bikes pulled up and Jack saw the men getting down and reaching for their weapons.

"Hold on!" Angus said.

He twisted the throttle and the engine screamed. The KTM shot down the track and back onto the rocky outcrop, it passed the bench and the warning sign, smashed through the wooden fence and soared at an angle across the waterfall. Jack's feet flew off the footrests and he found himself in midair clinging to Angus's torso, twenty metres above the waterfall. For some strange reason, a helpful motivational tip that Angus had once given to him on riding a motorbike floated through his mind:

Remember – when you're in the air, it doesn't hurt…

Jack had no time to be frightened. With an almighty crunch the rear wheel hit the track on the opposite side of the waterfall. Then the front wheel touched down. They had made it. Angus hit the front brake and then the rear a split second later. As he did so both tyres lost grip on the loose surface. Suddenly, the bike, Jack and Angus were sliding horizontally along the ground. They came to rest twenty metres on, when their forward momentum was finally interrupted by a giant slab of rock that rose up beside the track. Jack had been thrown free, but Angus was stuck under the heavy bike. Jumping to his feet, Jack rushed over to Angus. He reached down and tried to heave up the machine. With difficulty, he managed to pull the bike aside and he peered down at Angus's mud-caked body. The side of his face was badly scratched from where it had scraped along the track.

Angus was not moving.

Intruders

Jack shook his friend hard, but there was no response. He glanced behind him. The men had got off their quad bikes and were standing at the top of the rocky outcrop from where Angus had launched the bike. Slack-jawed, they stared down at Jack and Angus way below. They could not believe their eyes.

Suddenly Angus opened an eye. Then both eyes. He blinked and then he grinned. "That's what I call big air… let's do it again, but with the camcorder."

"One day you're going to get us both killed."

"Are they still after us?"

"They're back up there… I don't know if they are planning on shooting or clapping. Anyway, your madness has given us at least five minutes on them."

"If the bike starts."

Angus remounted the bike. The engine fired first time. He grinned.

"Houston – we have ignition and main engine start."

Jack rolled his eyes.

Ten minutes later they were safely onto the valley floor and back on tarmac heading down the single-track lane that looped round the back of the big Soonhope School estate.

"Stop!" Jack thumped Angus on the back and he pulled up.

Jack took out his phone. He had another message from VIGIL:

Rendezvous at VIGIL Emergency Entrance Two.

"Where is Emergency Entrance Two?"

"I remember it from training. It's in the parkland to the west of the school. We're only about half a mile away."

"But if there is some sort of raid… is it safe?"

"It's safer inside VIGIL HQ, with all their high-tech security stuff, than outside. Anyway, those are the orders. Ditch the bike and let's cut into the woods here."

A moment later, they were making their way through the dense woodland that fringed the school. They had been taught the main features of the VIGIL HQ security systems and roughly knew the network of underground facilities beneath Soonhope School. It included three emergency exits, which were secreted in various parts of the surrounding parkland.

"I'm sure it's supposed to be around here somewhere…"

Suddenly they heard a voice behind them. "Looking for something lads?"

Jack swivelled round.

Two familiar figures stood before them – their old friends, Tony Smith and Gordon Macfarlane – part of VIGIL's elite security team. They looked worried.

"What's going on?" Jack asked.

"A Revisionist assault on VIGIL personnel. We had the usual remote security detail keeping an eye on you up at Angus's farm at Rachan, but something's happened. Their comms are down.

We need to take refuge inside VIGIL."

Tony reached inside his pocket and pulled out a control device. He pressed a button and a small area in the undergrowth suddenly cleared, to show a circular metal covering set, a bit like a large drain cover, in a concrete base.

"Step back." Tony pressed the device again and the metal cover formed an aperture in the ground, revealing a steep spiral staircase leading downwards. It was illuminated by a blue glow.

"All clear, on you go…"

One by one, they stepped onto the spiral staircase. The steps began lowering automatically. As they dropped beneath ground level, the aperture closed silently above them, and after a couple of minutes they came to a gentle halt. Ahead of them was a door. Tony pressed the device again and it opened onto a short metal-clad corridor lit by the familiar dim blue glow. At the end of the corridor was a circular door with five letters etched on it:

V I G I L

The door opened without a sound, revealing a tubular passageway beyond. There were no markings on the passage walls – no rivets, no seams – it was completely smooth. They moved quietly through the entrance, which resealed itself silently behind them. It was like the inside of an Egyptian pyramid. They started to make their way along the passage.

Tony spoke into his mouthpiece, "Smith approaching Inner Hub. We have Jack and Angus. They are safe. Confirmed safe. Authorisation to proceed to Control Centre."

Tony's face drained of colour as he listened to the response on his radio.

He turned back to Gordon, Jack and Angus. "It is not looking good. There are intruders on the upper levels…"

"What?" Gordon said. "But that's impossible."

"We've taken casualties as well," Tony added. "Everyone is retreating to the Inner Hub – at least we should be safe in there."

At the end of the corridor there was a final large circular door, like the entrance to a bank vault. Tony looked up at the closed-circuit-TV system and whispered into his mouthpiece again, "Request access to Inner Hub."

Again, Tony went through the security procedures and the door opened. In a minute they entered the main Taurus Control Centre.

"Glad you are here, gentlemen."

It was Councillor Inchquin – the Chairman of VIGIL. Next to him stood the Rector, VIGIL's second in command. Both men looked more worried than Jack had ever seen them. There were two other men in the Taurus Control Centre. Jack and Angus's friend, Professor Gino Turinelli had his eyes fixed on a closed-circuit-TV monitor and Theo Joplin, the chief VIGIL historian, was tapping manically at a computer terminal.

"What's our position?" Tony asked.

"Not good," the Rector spoke gravely. For a moment there, all our systems were overridden; we had no communication. They've just come up and it seems that we have four men down on the upper levels. I don't even know if we were in time to warn all off-site VIGIL personnel and their security details. Look…" he waved them over to a large screen that showed a plan of the VIGIL complex. He tapped on the keyboard and CCTV footage popped up showing views of various parts of the building, including the maze of underground corridors. "We still have two small groups on site, but they're outside the Inner Hub – and their comms are down. The intruders seem to be able to move through the complex at will – it's as if they know all the security systems and can override them as they please…"

Jack spoke, "What about Mum – do you know if she's OK?"

The Rector turned away from the console and looked at Jack, a worried expression on his face. "No news yet Jack…"

"Joplin, have you managed to make any more progress on the scenario?"

"Christie did not have all the details, but he gave us what he could. A Second World War intervention – 1940. We're waiting to hear more from him… that's assuming he can contact us."

"It was Dad who sent us the first warning… up at Rachan," Jack said. "Does he know why this is happening?"

"Your father has done us a big favour," Inchquin replied, "but I suspect he's more concerned for your safety than ours…"

"What do you mean?"

"He has got wind of a Revisionist plan to intervene in history. He says it was something that he and Pendelshape used to talk about a lot in the old days… how to stop the Second World War."

"Does that mean that Pendelshape is still alive – he didn't die at Gravelines?" Angus asked.

"He would seem to be very much alive. He must be behind this. As soon as he knows that VIGIL has been defeated and our Taurus is under their control, the Revisionists will execute their plan."

"... and this time we won't be able to do anything about it," Jack said.

"Correct Jack. Not without our Taurus. We have to prepare to leave."

"What do you mean, leave?" Jack's brow furrowed.

Inchquin tried to keep his voice steady, but he wasn't finding it easy. "What I mean, Jack, is that we have Revisionist intruders. They are already inside VIGIL and seem to have control of our security systems. They are aiming to break into the Inner Hub – and then in here – the Taurus Control Centre. If they do, well, that's the end of VIGIL – and of us. The Revisionists will have no hesitation in killing us all and they will have a free hand to do what they want. Fortunately, the Taurus systems are isolated from the others. It gives us a breathing space. A final option..."

"Escape using the Taurus," the Rector said.

Jack was incredulous. "But... if we time-travelled out of here and then they destroyed the Taurus there would be no way of returning. We'd be stuck."

"It would leave us with one chance. We just might be able to intercept the Revisionists in 1940 and stop whatever it is they are trying to do..."

Jack looked over to the far side of the Control Centre where the Taurus sat brooding behind its blast screen, nestling within its arrangement of complex pipes, cables and access gantries.

"The Taurus becomes a lifeboat, then?"

"...and our only way to stop the Revisionists," Inchquin said.

"Gentlemen, I fear that it is time to prepare for the worst; prepare to go back to 1940." He looked at Jack and Angus, "and that includes you two."

Within minutes, they had changed clothes in the VIGIL transfer preparation area, gathered what provisions they could and loaded them into the special VIGIL backpacks. Already the powerful generators that powered the Taurus were starting up. Jack could feel his heart pumping in his chest.

"What space–time vector are we setting?" Joplin asked.

Inchquin sighed, shaking his head, "All we have from Christie is London, June 1940. Go for that. Gino – prepare the time phones and lower the blast screen. Taurus will be powered up shortly."

"Comms is back up!" Tony announced, one hand cupped over his ear. "It's Belstaff and Johnstone! They say they have managed to defeat a group of intruders on the second level and they're coming through to help us."

Inchquin clenched his fist. "Yes," he hissed. "It might not be over yet…"

"They're nearly here – outside the Control Centre. Shall I open the door?"

"Do it."

The heavy door at the far end of the Control Centre swung open and through it marched Belstaff and Johnstone. Like Tony and Gordon they were part of VIGIL's security team, but as they marched into the Control Centre, Jack could see from the looks on their faces that something was wrong. Very wrong.

Johnstone barked an order, "Everyone on your knees!"

For a moment, they did not understand the command.

But then Johnstone fired a volley of automatic fire into the ceiling.

"Do as I say!"

"What are you doing?" Gordon boomed.

But Johnstone's response was instantaneous and deadly. He levelled his weapon directly at Gordon and fired once. The round ripped into Gordon's chest and he was hurled backwards.

They all dropped to the floor.

The Rector looked up at their assailants. "What is the meaning of this?"

"Never you mind – just do as I say."

Jack knelt next to Angus. The situation was desperate.

"We're going to tie you lot up and then finish clearing the complex. Do exactly as you are told."

"Traitors! You swore an oath of loyalty to VIGIL," Inchquin seethed through his teeth. "We've still got others on the outside… you don't stand a chance. Give up now."

Johnstone laughed, "Everything's taken care of. I'm afraid it's all over for you lot, sir. We have already started Phase Two."

Jack glanced behind him at the Taurus – it was only five metres away and the blast screen was already down. The word he had used a few seconds before flashed through his mind again:

Lifeboat.

Surreptitiously, he caught Angus's eye and nodded towards the Taurus as Belstaff and Johnstone started to tie up the others. It was only half a chance, but it was all they had.

Jack whispered out of the corner of his mouth, "When I say 'go' you hit the blast screen control, I'll grab the time phones…"

Angus looked back at Jack with a glint in his eye.

"GO!"

Jack and Angus dived towards the Taurus. Johnstone looked up, levelled his weapon and fired without hesitation. But Jack and Angus were already halfway across the room and Angus had already thrown the blast screen control switch. The giant window accelerated upwards from its housing in the floor and the bullets ricocheted uselessly off it. Jack grabbed two of the preconfigured time phones nestling in their pods. He initiated the synchronisation procedure and set the countdown to fifteen seconds. They scrambled up the entry gantry into the waiting Taurus.

In front of them, the small heads-up display was already counting down:

12... 11... 10...

Around his feet, Jack saw shimmering eddies of light. The atmosphere within the Taurus structure was also changing and, outside, the Control Centre appeared darker and fuzzier. Jack could make out Inchquin, the Rector and the others looking up at them and the prostrate body of Gordon lying to one side. Belstaff and Johnstone were battling with the blast screen control panel and suddenly it started to come down. They raced towards the Taurus... But the countdown continued relentlessly.

7... 6... 5...

Belstaff stopped, aimed his weapon up at Jack and Angus and fired. Jack saw the spent rounds spit from the side of the weapon.

In their position up on the transfer platform, Jack and Angus were sitting ducks. Jack recoiled, waiting for the bullets to rip through his flesh. But then something extraordinary happened. Jack could actually see the bullets as they entered the atmosphere of the Taurus Transfer Chamber. Miraculously, the bullets slowed down, as if they had entered a jar of treacle. As they slowed, they distended until they looked nearly a foot or so long. In a moment they stopped completely and just hung there in the air of the Taurus Transfer Chamber. The nearest was only millimetres from Jack's heart.

Below, Johnstone clambered up the Taurus towards the Transfer Chamber. If the bullets couldn't kill them, he would physically drag Jack and Angus from the machine. In seconds he was there. He reached into the Chamber, but he was thrown from the Taurus and back into the main Control Centre, as if seized by a massive electric shock. He landed awkwardly.

Suddenly, at the far end of the Control Centre, Jack saw a new figure appear in the doorway. The man looked oddly familiar. Behind him, there was a teenage boy with blonde hair. The boy looked up from his position in the doorway to where Jack stood on the Taurus transfer platform. Their eyes met. Jack gasped in astonishment. The boy staring up at him looked exactly like… well, he looked exactly like *him*. In fact it *was* him.

3…2…1

Beneath Jack's feet, the flashing electrical whirlpool vanished and they stared down into a black abyss.

Pigeon Problems

Jack blinked as the rays of a dawn sun rose into a cloudless sky. He was sitting up and leaning against a curved wall of stone. His body ached. Angus was sitting next to him. He looked OK, but for one thing – a fat pigeon was sitting on his head. Angus detected the presence of the unfortunate creature at about the same time as Jack. He reached up and splatted the bird, which flapped away in a flurry of feathers, squawking loudly.

"Stupid thing…" Angus tried to look down his back, "has it crapped on me?"

Jack forced a grin. "Don't think it liked the look of you."

"I'm sore – did we make it?"

"Yes. But I've got no idea where we are."

Jack stood up and immediately wished he hadn't. He quickly sat down again and pushed himself back hard into the wall behind him. They seemed to be perched on a narrow platform of stone jutting out from a very tall pillar, high above a city square. Jack's feet were close to one of the edges of the platform.

"What is this place?"

The square below contained fountains and four large bronze animal statues, possibly lions, lying down, around the bottom of the pillar. Jack looked up. Just above them was a huge statue of a man, which must have been nearly six metres high. The man gazed out across the city. He wore a broad admiral's hat and his left hand rested on the hilt of his sword. The sleeve of his right hand was pinned to his tunic. He had only one arm. It was the final piece of information that Jack needed to confirm where they were.

"Nelson's Column," Jack said.

"What?"

"The Taurus has dumped us on top of Nelson's Column. Him up there – that's Admiral Nelson and that down there – that's Trafalgar Square. I think the Houses of Parliament are over there somewhere, yeah, look…" Jack craned his head. "That's Big Ben. See the clock tower? We're in the middle of London."

"Then what are those, over there?"

Jack followed the direction of Angus's gaze. Some way off, a series of large grey objects were floating in the sky.

"I think they're balloons… you know, barrage balloons… to stop planes. It's 1940 – the Second World War – that was the space–time fix that Joplin set. I'll check our time phone."

Jack reached into a pocket in his under vest and pulled out the time phone from its pouch. He flicked it open.

Date: 26th June 1940
Time: 05.30 a.m.
Location: Trafalgar Square, London.

"Well that confirms it. Has the time signal gone?"

"No. Still bright yellow… that means we're not out of the woods yet. Johnstone and Belstaff, or one of their cronies, can still come back and get us. There's no knowing what they'll do if they find us."

"We've got other problems too. How do we get down off this thing?"

Jack crawled forward on his belly to the edge of the stone platform. There was nothing to stop them from falling off the edge. Lying flat on his stomach, he peeked over. His heart jumped into his mouth. It was a sheer drop down to the square below. What made it worse was that the stone platform overhung the main column. There was absolutely no way of climbing down. They were marooned.

"What's it like?"

"I wouldn't look if I were you." Jack felt himself starting to panic. "Angus – I've no idea how we can get off this… I guess we could shout, maybe the army could climb up or something, but I can't see anyone down there, it's too early – seems completely dead."

Angus smiled. "Didn't they teach you anything in VIGIL training? Be prepared. Here…"

Angus patted his backpack. For the first time, Jack realised that it was considerably larger than his own.

"I brought a few extra bits and pieces from the VIGIL prep room. I grabbed everything I could. I noticed these, you know, we were talking about the Battle of Britain with Dad and what with me doing my private pilot's licence… and remember last time the Taurus dumped us on top of a castle…"

Jack had no idea what Angus was talking about.

Angus opened the back of his pack. "Anyway, I got one for you too…" He pulled out a large black bag. "…And in that bit there are the harnesses… you strap them round like this. It's very lightweight."

Jack's heart sank as he suddenly realised what Angus meant.

"Parachutes. You brought *parachutes* with you."

Angus's mouth curled into a grin. "As I said – be prepared. Don't worry – it's easy. You just strap it on, jump off the edge and pull the ripcord… er, apparently. Like this…"

"But you've never done it before."

"What? Of course not," Angus tapped his temple with his index finger. "D'you think I'm bonkers?" Angus considered his last remark for a moment and added, "Look – think of it this way, if it all screws up, you're not going to know anything about it anyway."

"I feel better already."

Angus started to strap the contraption onto his back.

Jack looked on, "You're not serious?"

"Come on Jack… let me help you with yours…"

Soon Angus was standing on the edge of the stone platform. He turned round to Jack, "So, you coming? Or are you going to sit there all day, getting crapped on by pigeons?"

"But…"

"Get a grip, man, we don't have any choice. Belstaff and Johnstone could be here in seconds."

For some bizarre reason, Jack felt himself drawn along with Angus's mad plan and soon he was standing next to him on the plinth, staring into the abyss with a parachute strapped to his back. He had just been transported seventy years through time into a war zone, and now he was being told to BASE jump off the top of Nelson's Column. He didn't feel well.

"Jump and pull... nothing to it. Just before you hit the ground, pull in the control lines and flare the 'chute. Land on both feet, then roll..."

Angus had the patter of a professional – but Jack knew he was blagging.

"Sorry, Angus... I just can't do it."

"Look Jack, people do this stuff all the time. They do it for *fun*, for sport, so it must be OK."

"I can't..."

"Well I'm going. The more I think about it, the worse I feel... At least when I'm down there I can get help..."

Without another word, Angus leaped from the stone plinth. One moment he was there, standing at the feet of Admiral Nelson fifty metres up in the sky, next he was gone.

"Wait!" Jack shouted. But it was too late. Jack looked down. Almost immediately Angus's parachute flowered from his backpack into a giant white cross on a blue background – the Scottish flag. Jack shook his head. The parachute immediately broke his fall and in seconds he had landed.

Jack edged forward, but then he stopped. He still had the time phone. He took it out again and noticed that the yellow light was still on. Now he had to make another decision. If they kept the time phone then, just like Angus said, the Revisionists could still locate them. They could come back and find them and then what? On the other hand, if Jack threw it away, they were stuck – maybe marooned for ever in 1940. He had to make a choice. He could hide it. But where? Jack closed the time phone and placed it at the rear of the narrow platform, where it met the pedestal, which supported the giant statue. It wasn't a great place but there was no time to think of anywhere else. At least no one would find it there… and if Belstaff and Johnstone tried to time travel back to it, they would get the same nasty surprise that Jack and Angus had just had. They would be stuck up Nelson's column. At the same time, at least Jack and Angus would know where it was, although getting it back might prove a little tricky. Jack approached the edge of the platform again and looked down. He could see the smudge of Angus's white face beaming back up at him from the square. He was grinning and waving.

Jack gritted his teeth. He was not about to be outdone. He stepped forward into the abyss and plummeted earthwards. The adrenaline gave him the second of clarity he needed. He pulled the ripcord; there was a second's delay and suddenly he felt as if he was being flung upwards. He looked down; the ground was still accelerating towards him at an alarming rate. He closed his eyes and braced himself for the impact. Both feet hit the ground and it felt like his spine had been detached from his body. He rolled sideways and came to a halt. He was down.

Angus rushed over and hauled him to his feet.

"Incredible!" His face was pink with excitement.

Jack felt unsteady and, suddenly, his legs gave way.

"You all right, Jack?"

"Give me a couple of minutes."

Angus hauled in the two crumpled parachutes and repacked them into their bags.

"I'll get rid of these. Can't see we'll need them. You feeling any better?"

"I need to go and sit down – I could do with some food or something."

Angus looked around. "It all seems very quiet. Maybe over there… that looks like a hotel or something."

In a few minutes, they approached the impressive façade of the Charing Cross Hotel, just off Trafalgar Square. There was a restaurant on the ground floor and, despite the early hour, it seemed to be serving. Jack was still feeling shaky and he knew he needed to sit down for a bit.

The area in front of the hotel was fringed with sandbags. A sleepy-looking guard, wearing a tin helmet, which looked too big for him, cupped a mug of tea beside a makeshift sentry post. He nodded to them as they passed.

A few weary-looking travellers were huddled inside the restaurant. Angus and Jack found a quiet table beside the window that looked out onto the street. A white-coated waiter spotted them and approached. He had a strong East End accent.

"You're up early lads. What can I get you?"

Angus didn't need to look at the menu. "Er, can you do us a big fry up – you know a few eggs, bacon, a few sausages…?"

Angus's order made Jack feel even more queasy. The waiter looked at them, grimaced and exhaled loudly, making a sort of *psssht* sound. "You having a laugh, son? Haven't you heard? There's a war on. There are restrictions you know…" The waiter then bent down and spoke to them furtively behind his palm, "unless, you know, you've got an extra bob or two…"

Jack and Angus glanced at each other.

"Er, get us what you can for, er, a pound…" Jack said.

The waiter took a double take. "A *pound*?" he said, completely astonished. He waited and then said the word again, this time whispering it, as though he might be struck by a bolt of lightning for saying it aloud, "A *pound…*?"

Jack blushed and shrugged his shoulders. "Sorry – I mean, you know, a few, er, shillings…"

The waiter looked at them oddly. "I'll see what I can do." And with that he wheeled round and marched off.

Jack whispered to Angus, "Think I might have got my valuations a bit wrong…"

"Do we actually have any money?"

Jack padded his backpack. "Of course… VIGIL prep room has the lot – just as you said, Angus, 'be prepared'."

"How long will the money last?"

"A lot longer than I first thought."

Jack had started to recover and his thoughts went back to their escape from VIGIL. It was then that he suddenly recalled the strange apparition that he had seen at the entrance of the Taurus Control Centre. "Angus… just before we escaped, did you see…?"

"What?"

"I know there was a lot going on, but after Johnstone fell off the Taurus, I looked over to the entrance of the Control Centre. It was open, and I swear I saw, well, I saw *me*… and also there was a guy standing next to me…"

Angus looked at Jack as if he had gone mad. "You saw *yourself*?"

"I know you can't see clearly through the atmosphere of the Transfer Chamber… but yes… I'm sure… and I think the other guy standing there, well, I think it might have been *Dad*. It's ages since

I've seen him, but Mum still has photos round the house and stuff."

Angus's eyes widened in amazement, "I don't remember that – are you sure?"

"I don't know," Jack shook his head. "How could it be?"

Angus shrugged.

Jack grimaced, "And I tell you, I only saw us for a moment, but we didn't look too good... I mean we looked like we had been beaten up or bruised or burned or something..."

"Maybe you saw *future* you or something weird?"

"Don't know Angus. I guess that's good isn't it? I mean that there is a future me. But there is one thing bugging me."

"What?"

"Well," Jack paused. "I don't know if it means anything, but you weren't with us."

An anxious look flashed across Angus's face – but in a split second it was gone.

"Forget it Jack. We can't worry about that now."

"But if it was Dad and me that I saw back there, then, well, that must mean we meet Dad somewhere and it must mean maybe we get back home somehow... I don't know. It's all too weird." Trying to fathom the logical implications of it all made Jack's brain hurt.

The waiter reappeared. "Here you go, lads."

He placed two large plates of egg, bacon and sausage in front of them. He glanced around, furtively. "Er, three shillings please."

Jack dropped the coins into the waiter's hand and he slipped them into his pocket without making eye contact. They had made a friend for life.

"Very good of you, sir. Very good indeed. Men will say that *this was your finest hour.*" The waiter said, putting on a gruff upper-class accent.

"I'm sorry?" Jack said.

"You know lads, from Mr Churchill's speech. I know them all off by heart…" The waiter cleared his throat, stood to attention, put on a low, growling voice and announced, *"Let us therefore brace ourselves to our duties, and so bear ourselves, that if the British Empire and its Commonwealth last for a thousand years, men will still say: this was their finest hour."*

He grinned. "What do you think lads – not bad, eh?"

Jack was bemused. "Er, very good."

The waiter realised that the boys hadn't recognised his impersonation of Prime Minister, Winston Churchill, giving part of the speech he had made the previous week. He blushed and said quickly, "So, will you need anything else?"

"Maybe something to drink… tea?"

"Certainly – and I have a few old newspapers if you need to kill some time."

"OK."

The waiter rifled through some old papers stacked on the sideboard.

"You know, I'm going to keep a few of these, I think. Some day one or two of these front pages might be quite valuable. This one's from just a few days ago."

The waiter held up the paper so they could read the headline.

FRENCH SIGN ARMISTICE

Jack scanned the article.

> *In the same railway carriage in which the 1918 Armistice was signed to end the First World War, yesterday the French signed an Armistice with Germany to end hostilities in France. Three fifths of France will be occupied by Germany including key Atlantic and Channel ports...*

Jack looked up at the date on the newspaper: *23rd June 1940*.

"My boy has joined the army... trust you two will be doing your bit to fight the Nazis?" the waiter said.

"Yes..." Jack faltered. "I suppose we will."

The waiter put on his Churchill voice again, "We shall fight on the beaches, we shall fight on the landing grounds, we shall fight in the fields and in the streets, we shall fight in the hills; we shall never surrender..." He stopped and looked at Jack and Angus for some sort of approval, but they just stared up at him blankly. Sheepishly, he put down the newspaper and shuffled off.

Jack flicked through the newspaper, "This makes pretty depressing reading... all about the war, rationing, evacuation... take a look."

As Angus flicked through the newspaper, Jack stared out of the window. The street was a little busier now and there were a few taxis, cars and buses moving up and down the Strand. The people in the street had no idea that, within a few weeks, their city would start to endure months of terror bombings in the Blitz, whilst a few young pilots would fight a struggle for the survival of their country in the sky above them.

"Hey – look at this…" Angus pushed the newspaper over to Jack. He was pointing at a small article under 'Other News'. The headline read:

AMATEUR SCIENTISTS HELPING WAR EFFORT

Jack started to read:

> *The government will consult scientists to discuss what else can be done to support the war effort. Details are classified, but a spokesman for the War Office said, "The British Empire stands alone against Nazi aggression. We must look at all ideas, from whatever source, that might help us in the war effort…" It is understood that scientists from leading universities will continue to be engaged but now amateur inventors and scientists will be contacted as well, as the War Office leaves no stone unturned in the search for new ideas.*

Jack squinted at a small, poorly rendered picture of two men underneath the article. The caption read:

> *Cambridge physicist – Dr Petersen and amateur scientist – Dr Pendelshape – to be consulted by War Office.*

Jack did a complete double take – staring back at him from the page was Pendelshape; somehow he had survived the battle of Gravelines.

Number 32 to Northolt

" **I** recognise him." The waiter paused from clearing their plates, leaned over and stabbed a chubby finger at the picture of Dr Pendelshape.

"What?" Jack said with incredulity.

"Yes. My mate who works down the road at the Savoy says he's been staying there for weeks. Must have a bob or two. You get all the posh sorts down there and the top brass – government, military – we're right close to Whitehall, we are." The waiter shrugged, "He's probably still there."

"What – at another hotel – what did you call it?"

The waiter peered closer at the picture. "Yes. I'd swear it's him. Yeah – the Savoy – just a bit further down the Strand, on this side. Only my mate mentioned it 'cos he tips well he does, a bit like you lads. Anything else for you, now?"

"No. But take this anyway." Jack thrust a pound note into the waiter's hand. "You've been very helpful."

The waiter stared, dumbfounded, at the one-pound note in his hand.

"Er, thanks – very good of you. Very good indeed."

The waiter moved off again with a spring in his step as Jack reread the newspaper article.

"We've hit the jackpot. Pendelshape… he's here… in London. It's exactly what Inchquin was talking about," Angus said.

"Jackpot in one sense, I guess," Jack said. "But if Pendelshape is here, well, it must mean that VIGIL has been defeated. Pendelshape wouldn't risk it unless he knew VIGIL couldn't stop him. It means we're on our own. VIGIL's last hope."

Angus's face fell. "You're right. What do you think they're trying to do?"

Jack rubbed his chin thoughtfully, trying to remember what Inchquin had said. "Well, Dad told VIGIL that they were planning an intervention in 1940. And they're here – you know – in London. So maybe it is something to do with helping the British defeat Germany early on in the war. Avoiding all the horrors of the war – it's a typical Revisionist plan. They tried it with the First World War… now they're trying it with the Second World War."

"But how?"

Jack looked at the article. "According to this, it looks like Pendelshape is posing as some sort of scientist. I don't recognise the other guy in the picture – Petersen – but maybe he is, like, a real scientist from Cambridge University or something. Maybe he has something that will be useful to the British government in their fight against the Nazis. Who knows? But I guess it's not surprising Pendelshape's here, bang in the middle of London. It's the centre of government – 10 Downing Street, Parliament, Whitehall, all the government places – everyone who matters hangs out here."

"Well, I think we need to pay our old friend Pendelshape a little visit," Angus said.

"Yeah, I'm thinking the same. But it won't be as easy as that.

He's probably got other Revisionists working with him. And, well, they will know we've escaped. Maybe, instead of confronting him, we should spy on him… see what he's up to, who he's talking to… maybe then we can work out what's happening… and then…"

"What?"

"Stop them – for good this time."

Angus grinned. "You're beginning to sound just like me." He scratched his chin. "There's just one thing we've forgotten."

"What?"

"The time phone. Maybe we should ditch it?"

"I already did."

"Are you mad? It's our only way back."

"I had to make a decision. If the Revisionists have taken over VIGIL HQ they will just use the next time signal to come and get us… we'll be dead meat."

"Where did you put it?"

"Left it on top of Nelson's Column. Couldn't think of anything else to do with it. At least we know where it is… and that no one will find it."

"So long as you don't ask me to climb up and get it."

"Well, it might come to that. But now we've got another good reason to check out Pendelshape. He might be our only way out of here."

Cautiously, they made their way east down the Strand, away from Trafalgar Square and towards the Savoy Hotel. A couple of taxis rumbled past in front of them followed by an old-fashioned, red double-decker bus. More people were on the streets now –

office and shop workers and quite a few men and women in uniform. They all carried odd-looking canvas boxes on strings.

"What's in the boxes?" Angus asked.

"Gas masks, I think," Jack replied. "Anyway, stop gawping and concentrate. I think the Savoy must be down here somewhere…"

"Jeez!" Suddenly, Jack stopped in his tracks and hauled Angus into a doorway. "It's *him*!"

Sure enough, standing right in the middle of the pavement, only twenty metres ahead of them, was the unmistakable figure of Dr Pendelshape. He was looking away from them, down the street. By the way he checked his watch and tapped his foot impatiently, they guessed he was waiting for someone.

"Don't let him see you," Jack whispered.

"What do you reckon?" Angus said. "Shall I take him out?"

Jack rolled his eyes. "How exactly?"

Pendelshape glanced at his watch again and peered down the Strand and then back up to Trafalgar Square. Jack and Angus melted into the shop doorway, but there was nowhere to hide. As he looked up and down the street and continued tapping his foot, a large black car slid to a halt right in front of him. Its rear windows were tinted black. A swarthy, well-built man in a black coat got out of the back and then a second man got out of the passenger seat. For a moment, Pendelshape seemed to hesitate. There was an exchange of words and Pendelshape took a single step back, away from the car. The swarthy man quickly looked up and down the street, as if checking for something, and then, quite suddenly, both men grabbed Pendelshape and man-handled him into the back of the car. The whole thing took less than five seconds and Pendelshape was taken completely by surprise. The doors of the car slammed shut and it drove off into the morning traffic as if nothing had happened. Apart from Angus and Jack, no one seemed even to have noticed that there might have been some sort of altercation.

Angus was the first to speak, "It looked like those men were arresting him."

"Or kidnapping him," Jack said. "Angus, the car's getting away. I think we have to follow them… he's our only hope."

The car was heading for Trafalgar Square. Soon it would be out of sight and Pendelshape would be gone.

"Over there!" Jack waved Angus to a taxi that had just deposited its passenger outside the Savoy.

Jack rushed over and stuck his head in the cab, "Can you follow that big black car?"

The taxi driver looked Jack up and down suspiciously, "Well, son, I'm not sure…"

Jack pulled out a ten-pound note, "We've got money."

It seemed to do the trick. The taxi driver's face lit up, "Hop in."

The taxi pulled off and soon they had passed through Trafalgar Square and were trailing the car, with Pendelshape aboard, towards west London.

Jack leaned forward. "We don't want to keep too close… just follow so we don't lose sight of it…"

Jack caught the driver's dubious expression in the mirror.

"What are you two then… secret agents or something?"

Angus leaned forward this time. "Almost. We're time travellers and there's an evil time traveller in the car in front, but he's the only one who can get us home."

The taxi driver laughed. "Gawd… well as long as you pay me, what do I care?"

The two cars snaked their way onwards through London. Quite soon, they were in the suburbs.

"Where's he taking us?" Angus said.

"No idea… we just need to stay on his trail."

Suddenly, the taxi driver interrupted them. "I'm sorry about this lads, but there's some madman on a motorbike behind us. He keeps trying to overtake…"

Jack and Angus spun round on their seats. The traffic was thinning out, and, sure enough, a motorcyclist was trailing them. He had on large goggles and a helmet – though it looked more like a skullcap. A yellow scarf billowed out behind him.

"I'm going to pull in and let him through," the taxi driver said.

Suddenly there was a roar as the motorbike closed in on the taxi, and then, moved dangerously into the oncoming traffic to try and overtake. In seconds it was alongside the taxi.

The taxi driver was suddenly anxious. "He's going to kill himself and us too if he's not careful…"

"Must be one of your relations, Angus, some motorbike nut."

Angus smiled. "Yeah, you're probably right – probably Great Grandfather Ludwig on his way to the airport to fly his Hurricane."

The motorbike drove on and as he passed the taxi, Jack and Angus noticed to their surprise that the motorcyclist was indeed wearing an aviator's leather jacket over some sort of military uniform.

The motorbike veered in front of the taxi, narrowly missing it. The taxi driver twisted on the steering wheel and braked sharply.

The taxi skidded, slewing sideways. They were out of control. Suddenly, there was a loud bang as they skidded into the back of a double-decker bus that was standing at a bus stop ahead. Jack and Angus were thrown forward, but fortunately the taxi was not moving fast enough to cause them injury. In the distance, the motorcyclist had not noticed a thing. He powered on through the traffic into the distance, leaving only exhaust fumes behind him.

Angus was first to come to his senses. He clambered out of the passenger door. Jack followed. The taxi driver pulled himself free – he had been less fortunate and clutched his head where it had thumped into the windscreen. The traffic on the other side of the street had slowed to a stop and people were coming to help. Passengers were climbing off the bus and the driver and conductor were coming over to inspect the damage.

"What a mess," Angus said.

"I can still see the car… up ahead. Pendelshape's getting away," said Jack. "Come on!"

"What and just leave this…?"

"*Come on*, Angus, let's go!"

"How?"

"What about that?" Jack waved his hand towards the bus they had just avoided hitting.

"You're not serious."

"We haven't got time to argue – *they're getting away*."

Most of the passengers were already off, but Jack helped the remainder on their way.

"Everyone off! Road closed!"

Jack waved the passengers away, while Angus jumped nimbly

into the driver's cab and revved the engine. There was a loud mechanical grinding as he tried to engage first gear. The last passenger leaped from the platform at the rear and there was a sharp jolt as the huge machine lurched forward. The driver and inspector looked back in horror as their bus kangarooed away from the bus stop. Suddenly realising what was happening, the two men sprinted to catch up with their bus.

"Make it go faster!" Jack screamed at Angus, who was perched up in the cab ahead. The bus was crawling forward at an agonising pace.

"I'm trying, but this thing's got a gearbox like a bowl of Mum's porridge…"

There was another painful mechanical crunch as Angus discovered second gear and, with a belch of diesel smoke, the bus staggered its way up from ten miles an hour to a heady fifteen. The driver made a heroic leap for the pole at the rear of the bus. He caught hold, but couldn't run fast enough to jump onto the platform. As his hand slipped down to the bottom of the pole, he clung on desperately and was dragged along the road.

"I'll get you, you little…" the driver spat through his teeth as Jack loomed over him.

Jack looked down in alarm as the driver pulled himself forward and managed to wrap his right arm around the pole. He was going to try and climb back on.

"Sorry, sir," Jack said, "we're commandeering your bus in the interests of, er, national security…"

Jack didn't like what he was about to do, but he knew he didn't have much choice. He kicked the bus driver's elbow hard.

The driver yelped and lost his grip, then tumbled back onto the road. Jack looked on as the man pulled himself to his feet, clenched his fists and screamed a string of expletives as the bus lumbered on.

Jack rushed to the front of the bus, where Angus wrestled with a giant steering wheel. He sported a huge grin.

"All clear back there?"

"Someone refused to pay, but he was good enough to get off..." Jack looked through the windscreen. "Can you see Pendelshape's car?"

Angus nodded. "Yes – they're up there... I'm just managing to keep up. No sign of that motorbike guy, though. What a lunatic!"

"Have they noticed us?"

"Don't think so. What are we going to do – just follow them?"

"It won't be long before the driver tips off the police or something and then we've had it."

The number thirty-two rumbled on, with Angus at the wheel. The suburbs had already thinned out and now they were in open countryside.

"He's going faster now. Where's he taking us?"

"Well I hope we find out soon, because I think we're in trouble."

Jack looked down towards the rear of the bus. Behind them he could see a police car, its bell ringing out over the sound of the engine.

"Police."

"We can't stop – we'll lose Pendelshape. Hold on, he's turning in... there."

Jack looked out of the side window of the bus.

"It's an aerodrome. There's perimeter fencing and big hangers and stuff. I can see some aircraft parked up. Look – they're letting Pendelshape's car through…"

Angus slowed down. They watched as the black car pulled up to a sentry box which guarded a large gate. Sandbags were stacked up all around. The sentry leaned in to the car and then stepped away. The gate started to open. They were only a hundred metres from the aerodrome gate as Angus pulled up. The arrival of a double-decker London bus was starting to cause some interest from the sentries and one of them left his post to walk up the road towards them. Just at that point, the police car pulled up beside the bus. Two burly policemen got out.

"Switch off your engine and get out." Jack stuck his head out of the window.

"Officer, there's a man in the back of that car – we think he's been kidnapped, er, or something."

The red-faced policeman yelled at them through the side window.

"Don't give me a cock-and-bull story… you two are in serious trouble – now do as I say and GET OUT OF THE BUS!"

Jack looked at Angus, expectantly.

But Angus didn't need to be told. He gunned the vast engine of the bus. The whole thing started to shake as it shot off towards the aerodrome gate, belching black smoke. The sentry leaped to the side and the bus swung in to the entrance. It crashed through the gate, which was still partially ajar, and headed into the aerodrome. They did not have time to notice the helpful sign inside the gate which read: *Welcome to RAF Northolt*.

"Over there!"

In the distance, they could see a large, twin-engine, civilian aircraft with its motor running. The black car was parked nearby and a man was being lifted on a stretcher from the back of the car and towards the aircraft.

"That's Pendelshape. He's flat out. Something's happened to him."

Angus pointed the bus in the direction of the aircraft and it lumbered on across the grass of the aerodrome, leaving a trail of destruction in its wake. But that was nothing to what came next. Suddenly, the ground ripped open right in front of the bus and mud spurted upwards in a giant plume. Angus threw the bus sideways to avoid the crater, which had breached the ground directly in front of them. The bus lurched violently to one side, Angus corrected it, but swung the wheel too far and it veered in the opposite direction and then fell onto its side, scraping along the ground, before finally coming to a halt.

Touching the
Face of God

Jack was dazed. He touched his head and looked at his hand. Miraculously there was no blood. He looked forward. The windscreen of the bus had shattered and Angus was already climbing through.

"Come on!" he shouted.

Jack staggered forward and stepped through the windscreen into the open. Perhaps they should have stayed where they were. A squadron of Stuka dive-bombers screamed down, one after the other, pummelling the airfield and the surrounding buildings and aeroplanes. Then the Messerschmitt 109s came in, flying just a few metres above the ground, guns blazing. Jack saw a row of parked Hurricanes strafed. Then, one after another, the fighter planes exploded in puffs of black smoke and orange flame. Soon, the whole place was stinking of burning gasoline. Incredibly, one or two pilots on the ground had made it to their aircraft and were desperately coaxing their engines to life.

At the far end of the runway Jack could see the civilian plane preparing for take-off – with Pendelshape inside. It started to make its way along the airstrip, picking up speed. Incredibly, the plane remained cocooned from the maelstrom all around. It was as if it were somehow protected.

Jack and Angus dashed forward. Twenty metres ahead, a lone Spitfire bravely nosed its way towards the runway. So far it had avoided being hit. That was about to change. Jack saw a 109 swoop in low, strafing the helpless plane. Bullets ripped into the fuselage and the pilot slumped forward onto the controls in his cockpit. The Spitfire ground to a halt right in front of them, its engine still running.

"We need to help him," Jack shouted.

Angus clambered up onto the wing of the Spitfire and peered into the open canopy. The pilot groaned.

"He's alive! Get him out."

The pilot flipped off his helmet and mask and gasped for breath. Angus and Jack heaved him from the cockpit onto the wing and then manhandled him down onto the grass. An ominous dark patch had appeared on his leather flying jacket. Jack scanned the airfield for any sign of help, but the scene around them was one of utter chaos: people were running away screaming; smoke poured from a number of the buildings. But the attack did not let up.

"You all right?" Angus asked the pilot.

The pilot looked up at them and grimaced in pain. He couldn't have been more than twenty years old. "I'll be fine. It's only a scratch. Ambulance will be here soon."

He jerked his head towards his Spitfire. "If either of you are pilots – take my Spit and get one of those bastards for me…"

A hundred metres away, the civilian plane was just lifting off the runway and heading up into the sky. Jack and Angus looked at each other. If they stayed out on the open airfield they risked death.

Jack looked up at the Spitfire. "Do you think you can drive this thing?"

Angus clambered back up onto the wing and peered into the cockpit.

"It all looks exactly like the simulator, but we do have a problem…" He glanced down at Jack, still tending to the pilot on the ground. "It's going to be a tight squeeze. We'll need to ditch our packs."

Jack clambered up and looked over Angus's shoulder. "You'll have to kind of sit on me." Jack looked up to where Pendelshape's aeroplane climbed slowly up into the sky. "If we don't follow him now we'll lose him for ever and we'll never get home again."

Another pair of 109s screamed in over them, guns flaming.

"That's it – I'm not hanging round."

They squeezed in to the cockpit. Angus flung the canopy shut and took the controls.

"I hope you know what you're doing."

"Piece of cake."

But looking at the dials and levers in front of them, it seemed anything but a piece of cake. And Jack noticed another thing: the visibility was shocking. All he could see was the long nose of the Spitfire pointing up into the sky in front of them and the spinning propeller. Jack was squashed on one half of the pilot's seat with Angus's large frame plonked half on top of him. And for Angus, pressed up against the side of the cockpit, it wasn't easy to see the ground and tell where they were going. Undeterred, Angus put on the pilot's mask and helmet, found the control pedals with his feet and grabbed the joystick.

Spitfires in flight

"I guess we head for the runway," he shouted, as the Merlin engine roared and the whole machine jerked forward.

"Ooops – bit too much."

"I think you'll have to weave around a bit so you can kind of see where you're going."

In seconds they were on the runway. Jack scanned the sky through the canopy.

"Is the raid stopping? They seem to be wheeling away…"

Angus was too busy to pay any attention. "Right, we're ready, bit of power, flaps, er, other important stuff, and…"

"Don't you have to say 'chocs away' or something?"

Suddenly, the noise from the mighty Merlin engine crescendoed and black exhaust blew from the pipes on either side of the engine cowling. The airframe shook as they surged forward, then bumped along the ground, faster and faster. Angus increased the power again then, miraculously, they were airborne.

"You're going left! You're going left! Straighten up!" Jack shouted.

Angus overcorrected and they veered right. After a couple more wild corrections, they straightened up: Angus was in control.

"Yes!" he shouted in exhilaration. "Come on!"

"That sign," Jack shouted, "says 'wheels down' – you need them up, don't you? Get them up. Up!"

"OK, OK, I know how to do that." Angus pulled a lever and the sign changed to 'wheels up'.

They heard a clunk under the aircraft.

"More throttle."

The Merlin responded again with a great roar and Jack felt

himself being pushed back into the seat as they surged forward, with Angus still half sitting on top of him. Soon they were hammering up strong and steady into a cloud-dappled sky.

"*Red Two, Red Two, this is Acorn Leader, glad to see you have finally decided to join us.*"

"I've got someone talking to me on the radio in my ears," Angus said.

"*Red Two, yes, you idiot it's Acorn Leader, we are ordered to follow but not engage, repeat NOT engage until we have reinforcements...*"

Angus pulled the mask from his face. "I've got someone called 'Acorn Leader' babbling something on the radio – what do I do?" Angus shouted back to Jack.

"Ignore him – we're trying to keep on the tail of Pendelshape, can you see him yet?"

Angus levelled out. The altimeter indicated just over seven thousand feet. Below them, Jack could see the rolling English countryside and already, not far beyond, the sparkling grey-blue of the English Channel.

"Over there!" Jack shouted. Sure enough, about half a mile away, they could see a cluster of aircraft in the sky. In the centre they could make out the larger outline of the civilian aircraft looking like a fat bumble bee. It was surrounded, above, below and on each side by the 109s and the Stukas that had just completed the devastating surprise raid on the Northolt base.

"Looks like Pendelshape's plane is being escorted by all those fighters," Angus said.

Jack thought for a moment. "We need to follow – but keep a distance – can you do that?"

"Yes – I think so."

The radio crackled in Angus's ears a second time – this time the voice was different.

"Acorn Leader this is Red One, over."

"Red One – Acorn Leader here, delighted you have joined us. We are to follow but await reinforcements before engaging..."

"Acorn Leader, I am terribly sorry but I must protest in the strongest possible terms... I do believe that our foe is planning further mischief and I would like to propose a course of action to dissuade him from this intent..."

"Shut up Red One."

"Thank you for your thoughtful suggestion, Acorn Leader, however, I would like to add that my morning constitutional has been rudely curtailed by the action of our enemy and I feel it necessary to indicate my sincere displeasure..."

"Red One – get off the R/T – we are to wait backup – do not engage, repeat do not engage."

Angus half-turned to Jack. "You should hear this on the radio – someone called Red One, I think we're called Red Two, he wants to attack, but the leader guy is not letting him..."

The voice of Red One came over the radio again, *"I am terribly sorry, Acorn Leader, my radio seems to be playing up somewhat, I understood you to say 'engage the enemy... engage'. I do declare that is a most capital idea and shall engage forthwith. I am your humble servant. Tally-ho! Tally-ho!"*

Although Angus could hear the radio transmissions through his helmet, he had no idea where either 'Acorn Leader' or 'Red One' were. But suddenly, from below and off to their left, a lone

Hurricane screamed past them and banked sharply right to pursue the swarm of German planes ahead.

"There he goes! Red One... he's mad... he's totally outnumbered. They'll crucify him," Angus cried as he banked their Spitfire into a more gentle turn and raised the throttle a notch to pursue Red One.

"Don't get too close, Angus, we don't want to get into trouble..." Jack said.

Angus could hear Acorn Leader screaming down the radio, *"Red One – Disengage! DISENGAGE! Red Two – do not follow, repeat await support, AWAIT SUPPORT!"*

Angus raised the mask to his face, "Er, yes, confirmed," Angus, still unsure of what to say, added, "your humble servant..."

Angus and Jack stared though the canopy, mesmerised, as they watched Red One steadily approach the English Channel and close in rapidly on the swarm of German aircraft. The German planes maintained a tight formation around the larger civilian aircraft, which forced them to fly at its much slower speed. It was becoming apparent that their role was to shield and protect the civilian aircraft with Pendelshape aboard, now he had safely escaped from the Northolt airfield. However, they had not allowed for Red One, who was closing in on them. Fast.

Red One picked an outlier from the central stack of planes and Jack saw a whiff of powdery smoke from his wings as he opened fire. Almost immediately, there was a corresponding puff of white from an enemy aircraft, and it arced slowly off its course towards the ground. Even though they were still some distance behind, Jack could clearly see the enemy pilot release his canopy and leap from the dying plane. He deployed his parachute, but it refused to open. Instead, a ten-metre plume of tangled cord and silk flailed wildly from the wretched pilot's shoulders as he plummeted earthwards. Jack stared on in horror. He knew they called it a 'Roman Candle' when a parachute failed to open in this way. Now he understood why – because that's exactly what the pilot looked like – a black stick, with a trailing plume of white parachute flapping high into the air above.

Two 109s now broke from the main fleet to deal with Red One, who, following his success, had already circled and was coming in for a second attack. He struck again – and a second fighter caught fire. This time, Red One did not get away so easily. The two 109s locked on to his tail and Red One threw his Hurricane into a series of violent twists and turns to try and break free. Jack and Angus edged closer to the melée. The main body of German aircraft either did not spot them or simply were not interested. Despite the unwelcome attention of Red One, they seemed intent on getting across the Channel with the civilian aircraft intact as quickly as possible.

"He's shaken them off!" Angus shouted.

Ahead, Red One had rid himself of the pursuing 109s, but incredibly, instead of giving up, he looped up and over and for a *third* time swooped back into the swarm, guns blazing.

"He's going in *again*," Angus said, awe-struck. "This Red One guy's a maniac…"

Red One came out of his attack empty-handed but once again was tracked closely by the two 109s. This time there was one important difference. "They're heading straight for us! Do something!"

Angus flicked the gun button to fire. But the combined closing velocity of Red One and his pursuing 109s with Angus and Jack's Spitfire must have topped five hundred miles an hour. In three seconds there would be a head-on collision. At the last moment, Red One pulled up and the belly of the oncoming Hurricane flashed over their canopy with centimetres to spare. But the 109s were right on his tail. Their guns flashed. Jack closed his eyes as Angus stabbed his thumb on the fire button. Their machine guns fired in a staccato burst that sounded like tearing Velcro and the cockpit filled with the smell of cordite. The first 109 flashed past almost scraping the roof of the Spitfire, followed seconds later by the second, which flew even closer. Jack opened his eyes. They were still alive.

"I believe that is what they call a close shave, Red Two, but I do declare you have damaged him… he's turning for home…" It was Red One on the radio. *"Acorn Leader, if you are still there, may we trouble you for a little assistance?"*

"I couldn't leave all the fun to you, Red One, second snapper is a confirmed kill."

"Capital, Acorn Leader."

Suddenly, Red One appeared close up on their left wing. Then a second fighter appeared on their right wing. Jack assumed that this was 'Acorn Leader'. Jack could quite clearly see both pilots from their cockpit. Jack noticed that Red One had a yellow scarf wrapped round his neck… just like the motorcyclist who had overtaken them in the taxi.

Acorn leader's voice came over the radio again. *"You disobeyed orders, Red One…"*

"Humblest apologies, Acorn Leader."

"... but it's the bravest damned thing I ever saw, Ludwig. You're forgiven. But don't do it again. Now let's pancake before our luck runs out..."

Red One gave a quick thumbs up, then banked sharply and was gone, swiftly followed by Acorn Leader. Jack and Angus were alone once more with only the sound of the Merlin engine pumping in their ears.

"Jack, on the radio just now, Acorn Leader – he called Red One a name. I think he said, 'Ludwig'."

"That's your great grandfather's name isn't it?"

"Yes. You don't think...?"

"Maybe, Angus... maybe you just saved your grandfather's life."

Ahead, the German convoy ploughed onwards. Jack looked down. Through breaks in the thickening cloud, he saw a long slither of yellow beach stretching into the distance. They had crossed the English Channel and were now above France: occupied territory.

"Angus, we're over France. I think we need to turn round."

"But I can still see them ahead – looks like they're descending."

"It's mad to continue. If we follow them and land we'll get captured... or, more likely, we'll get shot down or something. Come to think about it this was a completely bonkers idea in the first place."

"Might not be as easy as you think. Weather's closing in. It seems much uglier over here."

Angus was right. The visibility over England had been patchy, but good enough. But as they crossed into France it got worse. It was as if they had passed into a cold front or something and in a short while they were flying between two layers of thickening cloud. Occasionally, they caught glimpses of the German convoy a mile or so ahead, but it was descending and soon it had ghosted into the cloud layer beneath.

"We've lost sight of them completely now…"

Specks of rain started to dot the canopy.

"Can't we go down?"

"I can try…"

Angus throttled back and let the Spitfire dip lower and soon they were skimming the top of the cloud layer beneath. He descended some more and suddenly it was if they were inside a ball of wet cotton wool. They were flying completely blind.

"Whoa!" Angus shouted. He immediately pulled up and poked the plane back above the cloud. "I don't want to do that again – couldn't see a thing in that cloud."

"I think it's getting worse."

The gap between the two cloud layers was narrowing and the light was diminishing.

"What about the instruments… can we fly on those?"

"It's not that easy, Jack… we don't know how low this cloud goes… we could find ourselves down at five hundred feet or something and then slam into the side of a hill…"

Suddenly, Jack felt very frightened. The elation from surviving the dogfight had worn off. He was aching and cramped in the stuffy cockpit. Flying in the cloud, with rain and low visibility and a poorly defined horizon was extremely disorientating. Angus had proved his worth as a pilot, but flying just on the instruments, with no visibility, took training, experience and confidence – not just a private pilot's licence and a few hours on a home simulator, however realistic it was. Even if they descended through the cloud base, they had no idea where they were and it wouldn't be easy to find anywhere to land. They could turn for home; but their airspeed had remained at a good two hundred miles an hour and now they were well over mainland France. They had no idea how far to turn to hit the right direction for home.

Angus was silent. Jack knew that by now he too must realise that their situation was desperate. Despite the cloud and rain, the Spitfire arrowed on, the big Merlin engine up front running strong and smooth with an unwavering hum.

Suddenly Angus said, "If we stay up here, we die; I'm taking us down."

The aircraft dropped into the thick cloud layer. Instantly the light dimmed and the rain on the canopy intensified.

"We need to watch that altimeter and watch our trim…"

The altimeter whirled round as they dropped through the cloud… three thousand, two thousand five-hundred, two thousand…

"Getting low now…"

"But still can't see a thing through this stupid cloud…"

One thousand five hundred… one thousand…

"Surely, it can't be much longer?"

"I'm easing level at nine hundred feet. I just hope there aren't any hills in this bit of France."

Jack's heart was pumping, they were now flying at just over

a hundred miles an hour through cloud that remained as thick as soup. They could only see a few metres in front of them.

"I'm slowing again and going to go down some more…"

Jack felt his stomach rise into his chest as the Spitfire lurched down again.

Angus let out a sudden cry. A second later, Jack saw it. Looming out of the mist only twenty metres ahead there appeared a massive metal structure. Jack felt himself lurch sideways as Angus, with only seconds to react, cut speed and flipped the aircraft to avoid a head-on collision. Too late. There was a horrendous scraping of metal on metal. Then… darkness.

A Tour of Le Tour

Jack tasted blood in his mouth. He opened his eyes. He was lying on his side in the cockpit and his whole body throbbed with pain. Angus was slumped on top of him, unmoving. The canopy of the cockpit had been shattered. Jack blinked and tried to understand where they were. He looked up. They were surrounded by a damp swirling mist, which limited visibility, but he could make out a complex tracery of interlocking iron girders rising high above them, disappearing into the cloud. He twisted his head round and peered down over the edge of the fuselage where it met the canopy at the edge of the cockpit. He felt his chest tighten in fear when he looked down. Below, the same strange structure of metal latticework disappeared down into an endless grey void of swirling mist. Jack could not see the ground. The fuselage of the aircraft seemed to have come to rest on its side, but was firmly wedged between at least two sections of interlocking girders. The wings had been ripped free in the impact. Jack had no idea where they were, but they were suspended in midair and the ground was nowhere to be seen.

The weight of Angus, lying on top of him, crushed him into the side of the cockpit. Was he dead? Jack poked his friend in the back with his free hand. Angus groaned, and Jack felt a wave of relief. But the relief turned to horror as Jack realised that the blood in his mouth was dripping from Angus's face. Jack could only see the back of his head – but it was clear that there was a lot of blood and that Angus was in a bad way.

"Angus – are you OK?"

Angus groaned again. Jack rocked himself forward to try and get a proper look at Angus's injuries. But it was hopeless. He was completely stuck, with Angus unmoving right on top of him. His legs and back were numbing under the pressure. He pushed forward a second time and suddenly there was a groaning and scraping of metal as the whole aircraft moved against the steel struts that held it precariously in place. Jack froze. If he moved – the whole aircraft also moved. It was unstable and if it dislodged, they would plummet earthwards and then there was no way they could possibly survive.

They were trapped.

Jack felt anger welling up inside. Anger at Pendelshape, anger at VIGIL, anger at himself for getting them into this situation. They were utterly helpless and, to his dismay, Jack could feel the breeze was beginning to freshen. That wasn't good. Wind whistled through the strange structure and its criss-crossing iron beams appeared and then disappeared as the mist churned and eddied all around. Then, off to one side, Jack saw something extraordinary. The mist cleared for a moment and, as it did, a very large piece of red cloth floated down only a few metres away from them. As it dropped to earth, it suddenly unfurled right in front of Jack's eyes to reveal a large white circle on which was painted a strange black emblem. Jack had seen this particular emblem in scores of books and films and now it appeared in front of him like some ghostly warning. It was a Nazi Swastika. As quickly as the flag had unfurled before him, it wrapped itself back into a damp ball of red cloth and dropped out of sight into the mist below.

Jack was scared. He was in pain, his best friend was bleeding to death and there was nothing he could do about it, and now Nazi images were appearing, spectre-like, in the mist in front of him. Maybe he had died in the crash and this was hell. Finally, his eyes flickered and he passed out.

Voices. Very close. From his position he couldn't see anyone, but he could hear them. From out of nowhere a rope flopped onto the side of the fuselage and dangled into the canopy. Jack heard someone shouting at him, urgently, *"Ecoutez moi, on va vous lancer une corde. Mettez–la autour de votre taille. Dépêchez-vous, on n'a pas beaucoup de temps!"*

Jack didn't understand what they were saying, but he knew the language: French. And he knew enough French to reply.

He mustered his remaining strength and shouted at the top of his voice, *"Anglais! Je ne comprends pas!"*

For a moment there was quiet and then Jack heard a lively exchange somewhere above him. Then he heard another voice speak in good English with a strong French accent.

"OK my friend. We are going to save you. We will throw you a rope. You need to put the loop around you. Try and be quick."

Jack bellowed back, "There are two of us – I think my friend is badly injured…"

Again, Jack heard talking, and then the voice came again. "Stay calm my friend. We are coming!"

Jack whispered into Angus's ear – which was only a couple

of centimetres from his mouth, "Don't worry, Angus, we're going to get out of this…"

But Jack was not really so sure.

Then, just above him, Jack heard the voice again, suddenly much closer. *"Salut – mon ami…"*

Jack craned his head to try and see past Angus's slumped body. Just above him the face of a black man appeared, looking down through the mangled cockpit. He seemed to be floating in mid-air, somehow suspended from above. The man looked quite young, fit and entirely unconcerned that the ground beneath them was nowhere to be seen.

"I am Jean-Yves, and how do you say it in English? Delighted to meet you, old chap." He smiled. Something about the smile exuded confidence and it was infectious. Jack sensed hope.

"Thank God you're here. My friend, I think he is badly hurt, but he's breathing. Where are we?"

Jean-Yves shifted his eyes to Angus and Jack, a flash of anxiety in his face, but then he shook his head. "Your friend has cuts and bruises – a lot of blood. But he will be fine. Now take this rope…"

Jean-Yves worked the ropes quickly, moving with the speed and precision of a professional climber. He talked quietly to Jack as he worked, all the time speaking clearly, calmly. He could have been talking about the weather.

"You are very lucky to survive… what happened?"

"Er, we flew into cloud and lost our way…" Jack asked the question again. "Where are we?"

But it was as if Jean-Yves were deliberately ignoring the question. *"Incroyable.* Are you Royal Air Force… this is a Spitfire, no?"

"Was a Spitfire. Yes, RAF, we were in a fight over the Channel."

"But why are there two of you? This is a single-seater? And you, my friend, you look very young…"

Jack didn't have the energy to explain.

At last, Jean-Yves managed to secure one rope beneath Angus's arms and around his torso and a second around Jack. The plan was somehow to ease them free from the cockpit and lift them up to safety. Jean-Yves gave a slight exhalation in preparation.

"There… now we lift you up… OK?"

Jack tried a third time, "Where are we?"

Jean-Yves gave a half-smile. When he gave his answer Jack suddenly understood why he had ignored Jack's question until they were secured by the ropes.

"*Le Tour,*" Jean-Yves said.

"What?"

"*Mon ami*, you are two hundred metres up in the air, hanging off *le Tour Eiffel*." Jack detected a note of admiration in Jean-Yves's voice. For a second Jack did not quite get the rapid French pronunciation. Then it clicked into place. The Eiffel Tower. They had crashed into the Eiffel Tower – in the middle of Paris.

"Ready?" Jean-Yves asked.

Angus groaned as the rope tightened and he was pulled free from the wreckage. Jean-Yves guided his body as it was hauled upwards by his friends waiting above. Soon Jack could only see Angus's feet dangling above him.

"Now your turn, my friend. Focus on me. Don't look down."

Jack took a deep breath and felt the rope close like a vice around his chest.

"Use your hands to hold on to the rope."

Slowly, Jack felt himself being levered from the cockpit and hauled up into the air. His body spun slowly on the rope as he was inched upwards. He couldn't help looking down. As soon as he did, he felt nauseous, but he couldn't take his eyes away. The Spitfire was wedged between an array of metal struts that formed one edge of the upper section of the mighty Eiffel Tower. The wings had been ripped free and were nowhere to be seen. The rear of the fuselage stuck out slightly from the side of the tower and Jack could clearly see the little tail fin with its red, white and blue RAF insignia.

Jack dangled from the rope, swinging like a pendulum in the breeze. He closed his eyes and, bit by bit, was tugged upwards until, finally, he felt one arm and then a second enfold him and pull him up and over onto a metal platform. Angus was already on the platform and a young girl was leaning over him, dabbing at his face with a piece of cloth. Jack felt an overpowering sense of euphoria. Then, his legs gave way beneath him and he collapsed in a heap.

"Wake up, *mon ami!*"

Jack was lying on his back. Jean-Yves peered into his eyes whilst he patted the side of Jack's face with his palm. "You are OK now, yes?"

A bottle of water was thrust into his hand and then some chocolate. "Drink and eat, you will feel better."

Jack looked around. "Angus – is he…?"

But Angus was sitting up next to him. He had a bloodied

bandage around his head and held another dressing to his face.

"God – you OK?"

Angus's voice was shaky, "Feel like I've gone eighty minutes against the All Blacks. But apparently I'm fine. No breaks. Car, bus and now plane accident… all in one day… that's got to be a world record."

"We have to go now…" Jean-Yves said. "Or we will be in trouble. But first," he gestured to a tall, wiry blonde-haired man who was packing up the ropes, "this is Patrice…"

Patrice stooped and shook Jack by the hand, "Salut…"

"And this is Ours," Jack's hand was taken by a huge, swarthy man with short black hair. "Ours means 'bear', you can see why, no?" The bear flashed a toothy grin. "And this is Sophie, my daughter."

Sophie waved a hand in acknowledgement. She held herself with her father's poise and athleticism. She looked Jack straight in the eye with a challenging self-confidence, though she couldn't have been more than fifteen years old. She had a dark complexion and hypnotic brown eyes, and even though Jack was in a bad state, he stared at her longer than was probably polite. Jack noticed that Sophie had a small camera with her. It hung around her neck. Just then, she put it up to her face and took a picture.

"Sorry – Sophie – she likes to take photos. She is our official photographer."

Jack tried to smile. "Thank you. I mean, thank you for saving us… I am Jack and my friend is Angus. We're with the Royal Air Force, er…" Jack thought for a moment, "VIGIL Squadron."

"Well Jack. We are very pleased to meet you. Very pleased indeed. Now we go…"

"But – how come you are all here?"

"I know – you will have many questions… and we have questions for you… but we must move or the Nazis will come…"

Jean-Yves started to move from the platform to a very narrow spiral staircase. Ours and Patrice helped Angus, who was unsteady on his feet.

"Is this how we get down?"

"Yes Jack – a long way down. The lifts are not working…"

"Why not?"

Jean-Yves flashed him a smile. "We sabotaged them, *mon ami*. Hitler may have conquered France, but he will not conquer the Eiffel Tower. If he wants to get to the top, he will have to walk…"

"Is that why you're up here – to break the lifts?"

"Not only…"

Jack remembered the strange sight of the Nazi Swastika flag falling to the ground. "You have been to the top and taken down the German flag?"

Jean-Yves stopped on the staircase and looked back at Jack. He smiled. "You have a lot of questions, eh?" he shrugged. "But of course you are right. We took a chance while the weather was bad."

"So you are French, er, resistance?"

Jean-Yves gave a shrug. "Whatever you like to call us, Jack."

"And climbers?"

"Sometimes climbing, sometimes other things. We like, er, *les jeux abnormales* – running, climbing, tricks – the Eiffel Tower – it is a good place for it…"

"Like free running…?"

"I do not know what that is Jack... *c'est l'art du deplacement.* We call it Parkour..."

And with that, Jean-Yves jumped over the barrier of the spiral staircase with the grace of a leopard and landed feet first, a good three metres below, on a very narrow steel platform and looked back up with a broad grin.

"Voilá."

The manoeuvre would have crippled a normal man, but for Jean-Yves it appeared effortless. It looked like Jack and Angus's new friends might prove useful – very useful indeed.

Schutzstaffel Surprise

"*Chaud devant!*"

Bonaparte's was like Gino's but French. Very French. Three waiters in wine-coloured aprons criss-crossed the floor between booth and table, table and bar in an endless choreography of service.

"*Chaud devant!*" One of them shouted again, warning others to make way as he burst through the swing doors from the kitchen, a silver tray held high over his head. Many people had left Paris, but it seemed Bonaparte's would always pulse with life. It was mid-morning and all the window booths were already taken. Housewives in headscarves sipped coffee, a watchful eye on their baskets; some youths played a noisy game of cards, their table littered with crumbs and empty glasses and six students squeezed around a table for four, poring over a book.

At the zinc-topped bar, that ran almost the entire breadth of the room, a worker in blue overalls regaled his comrades with a story, one foot propped against the brass foot rail, his eyes squinting against the smoke that rose from the cigarette glued to his bottom lip. Behind the bar, with its gleaming beer pumps, stood the coffee machine, a dangerous-looking contraption of valves, taps and pipes that whistled and hissed and spat, releasing gouts of steam and a thin stream of fragrant black liquid into china cups that were instantly whisked away by the waiters.

Surveying the scene, like a general surveys the field of battle, Antoine, the proprietor, stood with his large, aproned stomach wedged against the bar as he rhythmically polished a glass – not because it was dirty, but because it was clean. As the proprietor of his own café, just like the famous Emperor that gave the place its name, frankly, he could do what he wanted.

As they entered, Jack saw Antoine give Jean-Yves the scarcest of knowing looks, followed by a barely perceptible nod of the head. Seconds later they had gone through to the back of the café, down through a hatch in the floor of the kitchen and into the cellar. Along one side stood rack upon rack of wine bottles. On the other side there were barrels of beer. Jack felt refreshed after a long night's sleep at Patrice's small flat, but he was still disorientated and his head, neck and shoulders still hurt. His body had taken a real pounding over the last twenty-four hours and he didn't think it could take much more. But Angus was in a worse state. He had taken the brunt in the crash, and although they had carefully dressed and redressed his wounds, he was still in some pain and winced when he moved.

Jean-Yves sipped his coffee. "You must eat, *mes amis*," he gestured to the breakfast laid out on a crude wooden table. "As much as you can." He shook his head. "You were very lucky… I still cannot believe it."

"You saved our lives, Jean-Yves," Jack said. "Thank you."

The words hung in the air for a moment.

"We were happy to help. It was an amazing escape. An incredible

The Eiffel Tower – collision in the clouds

story. Look – Sophie took this – she could not resist adding it to our collection."

Jean-Yves fished something out of his pocket and handed it to Jack. "She took it yesterday after the crash and then developed it at the flat. It's quite good."

It was a photograph of the Eiffel Tower taken from some distance. The top of the tower was in low cloud. Then Jack spotted it – the tail fin of an aeroplane sticking out of the tower just below the cloud line. He nearly jumped out of his skin. The photo was exactly the same as the one that Angus's dad had shown them at Rachan. He looked up at Jean-Yves, who grinned back.

"The plane dropped out of the tower soon afterwards, just before the Nazis arrived. They must be very confused about what happened to the pilot."

"Hopefully they'll never find out."

Jack stared at the photo again, mesmerised.

"Is this place, this café, a hiding place?" Angus asked, waving a knife in one hand.

"A meeting point," Jean-Yves corrected. "We are slowly building a resistance force. We call it the 'Network'. But it is dangerous. Since the defeat, people are confused – scared. Many have left Paris, they are still trying to understand what the surrender means. But they know if they don't do what the Nazis say, they risk their lives." Jean-Yves took another sip of coffee. "But we can help…"

Jack's brow furrowed, "How?"

"We have many friends…" he smiled. "My wife, Marianne, she works in the government… She has good contacts. It will help us fight back."

As he spoke, images from the Second World War that Jack had seen in books and films flashed through his head. He knew that they were only at the start of the war and it would go on for another five years. More than fifty million people would die, and France, like all occupied territories, would suffer horribly.

Jack looked down at his empty plate and murmured under his breath, "You have no idea how bad it will be…"

But Jean-Yves did not hear him. He looked at his watch. "Marianne should be here soon," he smiled at Jack. "She was very excited to hear about you. Two pilots – you can help us, for sure."

At that moment the hatch to the cellar opened. They heard muffled chattering from the café upstairs. A slim, dark-haired woman stepped down the steep staircase into the cellar. As she reached the floor of the cellar she stopped and stared at Jack and Angus. She was excited but also anxious.

"These are the pilots?" she asked. "You seem very young…"

"They survived – it is incredible."

"Two of you? In one plane? How?"

"Er, it's a long story," Angus said.

"We must plan to get you back to England. Pilots are valuable," Marianne continued. "The Network will help. But it may take some time… and we are busy with other activities. Maybe you can help us?"

Jack did not have any time ask what 'activities' Marianne referred to because, just at that moment, the hatch opened and her daughter appeared.

"Sophie – you shouldn't be here…" Jean-Yves said.

Sophie ignored her father, "Well I am…"

Jean-Yves could free-climb up the Eiffel Tower and probably the north face of the Eiger for all Jack knew, but he had clearly learned that resisting his daughter's will was fruitless.

Sophie continued, "I came down to warn you... Gottschalk has been spotted in the street. He is heading this way. I think we need to leave..."

They re-emerged from the cellar and slipped back into the café. Then they stopped in their tracks. A few minutes before Bonaparte's had been alive with noise and chatter. Now you could hear a pin drop. Everyone in the café was looking towards three men who stood at the bar. They wore grey uniforms and black boots and they were armed. But it was the man in the middle who caught Jack's attention. His uniform was trim and smartly tailored with two breast pockets and broad, upturned cuffs. At his throat he wore a black iron cross and on his right collar there was an emblem of two identical zigzags side by side, like lightning bolts. He wore braided shoulder boards and above the cuff on his left arm Jack could make out a black band with silver lettering which read 'Deutschland'. Above his left breast pocket there was a ribbon of red, blue and gold – like Jack had seen soldiers wear in place of medals. He wore a black belt, from which hung a holster for a side arm and a sheath for holding a dagger. The man was probably around forty and had a thin, pale face and penetrating green eyes. He was tall and his height was accentuated by a high-peaked cap. At the top of the cap Jack saw the stylised figure of an outstretched eagle. Beneath this, there was a final detail which confirmed the identity of the man before them. At the centre of his cap there was an unusual silver emblem. It leered out at them with grinning teeth – a skull and cross bones. It was called the *Totenkopf* – the Death's Head – and it was a symbol that personified pure evil. The man before them was an officer in the Nazi *Schutzstaffel*.

The SS had popped into Bonaparte's for a lunchtime drink.

Angus and Jack had missed the first exchange between the tall SS officer and Antoine, the proprietor of Bonaparte's, but clearly it had not gone well. Antoine's puffy face had turned bright red and his large double chin wobbled. Beads of sweat were starting to form on his forehead. Jack was only a few metres away and he desperately wanted to slide back into the kitchen and down into the cellar. But there was an edgy silence in the café and he quickly realised that any movement would draw instant and unwelcome attention.

The SS officer spoke again. He had a calm, polite voice, "Perhaps we will try again, *Monsieur?*" he smiled. "My friends and I would like three glasses of brandy."

The words hung in the air. Antoine's face flushed an even deeper shade of purple. He was being asked to serve Nazis in front of his friends and clientele. For Antoine it would be an act of humiliation and treachery. He was being put in an impossible position.

Antoine's voice cracked, "I cannot serve you…"

The SS officer did not react. He looked down at the end of his boot for a moment. He twisted his foot first one way and then another, as if inspecting the boot for any residual scuffs or dirt. He continued with this performance for a full ten seconds as if distracted or embarrassed by Antoine's brave words of defiance. Then he raised his head again and levelled his eyes at Antoine. Very slowly, the officer undid the holster at his belt and removed a black Luger. There were gasps from the onlookers and he saw one woman put a hand over her mouth to stifle a scream. The officer raised the ugly weapon so it was pointing directly at Antoine's head. Antoine started to shake and his chin wobbled even more. Slowly, the officer moved the barrel towards Antoine's forehead, wrapping a pendulous index finger around the trigger as he did so. Jack stared on, horrified. Then, the officer did something strange. Instead of pointing the gun at Antoine's forehead, he shifted its direction slightly and slowly moved it towards Antoine's left eye socket. Antoine gave a little gasp of fear. He closed his eyes tightly, but the officer eased the muzzle of the gun into the eye socket and rested it there. The idea of a bullet through the eye rather than through the head made the threat even more frightening, cruel and sadistic. Antoine started to sob. Jack wanted to leap to his rescue, but he knew to do so would mean instant death.

Suddenly, Marianne broke ranks from their little group at the kitchen door and marched forward. The SS officer and his two friends were taken aback by the sudden movement to their side and they wheeled round to train their weapons on her as she approached. For a moment it appeared as if she, instead of the hapless Antoine, would be gunned down in front of them. But Marianne flashed her most winning, radiant smile. She put up her hand and with an outstretched palm, gently waved the officer's Luger to one side, put a slender arm around his shoulder and manoeuvred him back to face Antoine and the bar.

"Gentlemen, gentlemen, please," she said breezily. "Have you not heard? The war is over and France and Germany are at peace.

We might as well all accept it and get on with our lives…" she flashed a knowing look at Antoine, still standing defiantly behind the bar. "Please make that four brandies… and I shall pay," she turned round to the astonished people in the café and lifted her arms in a gesture of reassurance. "Nothing more to see here!" she shouted, as Antoine dutifully poured the drinks and placed them on a tray.

It was as if someone had pricked a giant balloon. The tension from the room evaporated; people turned back to their drinks, food and chatter.

As Marianne escorted the soldiers towards a booth the students quickly evacuated. She put the tray, with four filled glasses, down on the table. She raised her glass, downed the rich dark liquid and banged it on the table. She glanced flirtatiously at the officer and his comrades, who, not to be outdone, downed their drinks. Marianne clicked her fingers over her head and a waiter came scurrying to the side of the table.

She smiled. "You might as well bring the whole bottle…"

And for the first time the SS officer smiled too.

From across the other side of the café, Jean-Yves whispered to Jack and Angus, "My wife's a brave woman – one of these days she is going to get herself killed."

"Who is that officer?" Jack asked.

"Axel Gottschalk," Jean-Yves whispered back to him. "A rising member of the SS. He knows Adolf Hitler personally. He is based in Villiers-sur-Oise, to the north, but he is often in Paris. He is an important target for us. I am not surprised to see him – particularly given what is happening over the next few days."

"Nasty piece of work…" Angus said.

"Yes," Jean-Yves replied, "he has something of a reputation. We must leave, before anything else happens."

But as they approached the main entrance of the café, the big glass door swung open and a man walked in. He was slim and wore a light suit and a dark tie. He was well groomed and his short, light brown hair was brushed back to show that it was starting to thin at each temple. He had a confident, authoritative air about him and he scanned the restaurant impatiently until his eyes came to rest on Gottschalk sitting with the two soldiers and Marianne in the window booth. He walked briskly over to their table. Gottschalk clearly recognised the civilian and invited him to sit down next to them. There was something oddly deferential about the way Gottschalk acted in front of the new arrival. It was particularly strange as one was an officer in a victorious army and the other seemed to be no more than a non-descript civilian. In contrast, Jack felt there was a self-consciousness about the civilian, a reluctance to be seen with these bullies from the SS. Marianne was now being introduced to the civilian and they shook hands. Soon she was in animated conversation with the four men and her eyes sparkled as she smiled and gossiped. They were putty in her hands.

"And who is that man?" Jack whispered.

"Albrecht Altenberg. He is a German scientist. A physicist, I think. Quite famous. He is seen with Gottschalk frequently here in Paris but also in Villiers. I think they are friends," Jean-Yves replied. "We must go. Marianne can handle it. Come on. Our place is not too far."

Jean-Yves continued walking to the door of the café followed by Sophie, Angus and Jack. Jack wanted to ignore Gottschalk, but somehow he just couldn't. He glanced over to their booth as he made for the door, trying hard not to walk too fast. Gottschalk spotted the movement from the corner of his eye and looked up. It was as if Jack had been caught in the cross hairs of an assassin's rifle. A shiver ran down his spine... he wanted to look away, but he found himself staring back. As Gottschalk looked at him, his expression changed. Initially, he seemed a little bemused at the sight of Jack, but then Gottschalk's brow furrowed. Finally, Jack turned. The door to the café was now only two metres away and he quickened his step, but his legs started to wobble and his stomach churned. He felt naked. It was as if not only Gottschalk was staring at him, but everyone else in the café as well. The big glass door was now only a step away – he reached out for the handle. Beyond it, he could see Jean-Yves, Angus and Sophie already melting away into the street.

"*Arretez!*"

Jack froze. He did not dare look round. For a second time in ten minutes the café was silenced. Approaching from behind, Jack could hear the heavy boots approaching slowly across the tiled floor. He could feel Gottschalk's eyes boring into the back of his head. The footsteps stopped.

"*Tournez-vous.*"

Jack could feel Gottschalk's breath on his neck – inches behind him. Slowly he turned round. Gottschalk looked at him.

"Name?"

Jack knew that one word from him and the game was up, but he was too terrified even to try and speak.

Gottschalk's eyes narrowed as he stared intently at Jack, "I asked you kindly to give me your name."

Jack felt his face burning red.

"Now, officer, please don't tell me we have another problem…?"

It was Marianne, approaching Gottschalk from behind.

Gottschalk half turned his head but kept his eye on Jack. "Nothing to trouble you my dear… I was asking this young man to be polite enough to tell me who he is and where he is from…"

For the first time, Jack saw fear in Marianne's face. Gottschalk looked into Jack's eyes and reached down to his holster. Once again, he withdrew the Luger.

"Now, let me ask you one more time. What is your name?"

Jack stared stupidly, paralysed with fear. Then, suddenly, help arrived from an unexpected source. The portly figure of Antoine appeared behind Marianne and the officer, carrying a silver tray in one hand. On the tray there was a large goblet of brandy.

"If you please, sir," he said.

Gottschalk half-turned, distracted. "What on earth do you want?"

"More brandy, sir…"

"Not now you fool – we are busy here. We already have what we need."

Antoine looked hurt, his puffy lips turned down in dismay. "But this is our very finest, Bonaparte's brandy, we would like you to try it, *Oberstleutnant*."

The officer looked at Antoine with extreme irritation.

"*Brigadeführer…*"

"Of course… I meant *Brigadeführer*."

Suddenly, with his free hand, Antoine reached into his pocket and withdrew a silver lighter. He deftly flicked it open and waved the lighted flame across the top of the glass. A blue flame burst into life as the alcohol caught fire. In a single smooth movement he dropped the lighter, took the glass and thrust it straight into Gottschalk's face. He screwed the glass round so the rim immediately shattered, lacerating the skin. The flaming brandy splattered everywhere. Gottschalk screamed. Just for a split second, Jack watched as Antoine's puffy face lit up in an expression of pure joy. It was the last thing he would ever do. Gottschalk held one hand to his bloodied, burned face, but the other still held the Luger. He lifted the gun to Antoine's head and fired without hesitation. Once.

Antoine's fat legs gave way and he dropped to the floor. Jack only had time to see Antoine's eyes staring unblinking at the ceiling, a small entry wound in his forehead and a pool of crimson growing ominously on the floor. The two other soldiers jumped to their feet... but Marianne was quicker. She brought her knee hard up into Gottschalk's groin and he doubled over in pain, his gun spinning from his hand. Then she stuck her elbow into the back of his neck and he groaned as he fell to his knees. The two soldiers raised their weapons but Jack and Marianne were both through the café door before the first shots rang out, shattering the glass of the windows and the door. Jack and Marianne raced down the street towards the safety of the Paris Metro, leaving Bonaparte's in chaos behind them.

No Regrets

"**Y**ou see what we are dealing with," Jean-Yves said bitterly. "The Nazis are murderers."

The atmosphere in the little apartment was grim. They had arrived at the safe house on Rue Le Regrattier only two hours before. The street was situated on the Ile St Louis – a small island in the middle of the Seine, only a short walk by bridge to the larger Isle de la Cité where the famous cathedral of Notre Dame stood. In contrast to the other fine apartments that looked out over the Seine from the island, the safe house was a little flat at the top of a higgledy-piggledy staircase. It had only one bedroom and its single front window looked over Rue Le Regrattier, straight into the apartments opposite. If you craned your head out through the open window to the left, you could just see the waters of the Seine languidly drifting past in the late afternoon sun.

Marianne had bought provisions from the *boulangerie* down the road, but food was the last thing on Jack's mind. He still felt sick from witnessing the cold-blooded murder of Antoine and exhausted from an escape through the Paris underground that had seen them switch from metro to metro, until Jean-Yves was completely sure that they had not been followed. They had picked their way back to the Ile de La Cité before finally coming up for air and slipping in to the old flat here in Rue Le Regrattier.

"We will avenge Antoine," Jean-Yves said once again as

he stomped angrily around the apartment.

Marianne stood up and put her hand around Jean-Yves's shoulders. "Jean – stay calm. It is already planned for tomorrow and, if that doesn't work, there is Villiers."

He sighed. "You're right, of course, my dear."

Jack had no idea what they were talking about. "What is it Marianne? What is happening tomorrow?"

Jean-Yves looked at him with fire in his eyes. "Tomorrow we change the course of history, Jack," he thought for a moment. "And the more I think about our plan, the more I think maybe you can help us."

Jack was none the wiser.

"The Germans have kept it quiet, but we know all about it," Marianne said. "Hitler himself will come to Paris tomorrow morning. He's coming to see his new conquest – coming to gloat."

"And we will be ready for him. We are going to assassinate him, Jack. We will stop this Nazi evil before it goes any further."

For a moment the words did not sink in. Then Jack felt a horrible sick feeling rising from the pit of his stomach.

"You're planning to assassinate Hitler, here? In Paris? Tomorrow? But…"

"We know exactly when he arrives and the route he will take. Everything is prepared."

Suddenly, Jack remembered the picture that Angus's father had shown them of Hitler standing in front of the Eiffel Tower. He'd told them it had been taken in 1940 – the only time Hitler had visited Paris. Jean-Yves and Marianne were talking about the same visit, Jack was sure of it. The photograph would be taken tomorrow, but as far as Jack knew, there was nothing in history about an assassination attempt during the visit. And of course, Hitler had not died until 1945 – five years later. That could only mean that whatever Jean-Yves and Marianne were planning, it would not turn out as they intended.

Jack took a deep breath. "Jean-Yves, I understand why you want to do this," he had to swallow back a lump in his throat, "but what you are talking about is very dangerous…"

"Of course it is dangerous. That doesn't matter. We have to act against this evil. We have our chance and we are going to take it." He paused for a moment. "And you can help us… Help Sophie, with the signalling."

"What?" Angus exclaimed. "Hold on…"

"You will not help us?" Jean-Yves looked surprised. "But we are allies and you are military pilots, it is your duty to help us, is it not? Intelligence like this is rare – chances rarer. We must seize the opportunity."

This was spiralling out of control. Not only was Jack worried for their own safety, but he was sure that the visit was a success. If there had been an assassination attempt it must have failed, or have been covered up. And if that was the case, what had happened to the assassins?

He battled to articulate his concern to Jean-Yves and Marianne. "It can't be that simple. You are talking about assassinating Hitler. He will be well guarded. And, well, even if you succeed, we don't necessarily know that the world will be a better place…"

Jean-Yves and Marianne looked at him, bemused.

With difficulty, Jack tried to explain, "I don't know, but even if you killed him – somebody else might take over. That somebody might be, I don't know, a better leader – he might even keep Nazi Germany in place for longer… maybe that would be even worse…"

"You're wrong, Jack. We all know that Hitler and his followers are criminals and that they have harnessed an entire nation to carry out their work. The Nazis are evil, Jack, pure evil. You saw Gottschalk – they are all infected in the same way. We must stop it. Anyone can see that. Hitler is the leader – and we will plan to kill him and hopefully Gottschalk and any of his other cronies at the same time. If we fail there is a back-up plan. A second cell. I don't want to be harsh with you, but we saved your lives and now we need your help. Then we can get you home."

There was silence in the room but for a breath of summer air that rose from the Seine and twitched the white cotton curtains that screened the windows. Jean-Yves, Marianne and Sophie were all watching for Jack's reaction. Until that point, Sophie had been brooding in an armchair by the fireplace, her arms folded around her knees. Suddenly she spoke, "Surely you must see that this is a good thing we are doing?"

Jack had no answer.

"Good. It's agreed then. No more discussion," Jean-Yves said. "He walked over to the table and unfurled a map. "Come – I will show you our plans." He pointed to a spot on the table off the map. "Hitler will arrive here at Le Bourget airfield, north-west of Paris at around five-thirty tomorrow morning. Three open-topped Mercedes sedans will be waiting. Hitler will probably sit in the front seat next to the chauffeur. Our information is that he will be accompanied by Albert Speer, his architect, and the sculptor, Breker. There will be adjutants in the back seats. They will first go to the Opéra. Afterwards, they will drive to Place de La Concorde, up the Champs-Elysées to the Arc de Triomphe and onto the Eiffel Tower…" Jean-Yves continued running his finger carefully along the route, "… then he will go to Invalides – to visit the tomb of Napoleon – and then back across the river to Sacré-Coeur. Our intelligence says he will be in Paris for no more than three hours. Then he will go on to Villiers-sur-Oise," Jean-Yves looked up at them with cold eyes. "This will be his last visit… anywhere." He stabbed his index finger into the map. "And that is where it shall be done…"

"The Arc de Triomphe," Marianne said.

"Well-named… and with twelve streets around it – there are plenty of escape options," Jean-Yves added.

Suddenly, there was knocking at the door. Three slow knocks, followed by three fast ones. Jack and Angus exchanged worried glances.

Marianne looked at her watch. "Eight-thirty. Ours and Patrice. Sophie – let them in. We will have supper and afterwards we will go through everything again."

An hour later they had finished their evening meal. Jean-Yves had opened a bottle of wine. Food and a glass of wine had taken the edge off Jacks' nerves. Jean-Yves pored over a map of central Paris and went through the plans with everyone again.

As he was finishing, Jack remembered something. "Jean-Yves, earlier you mentioned a back-up plan. What did you mean?"

"Yes Jack. Our intelligence says that after Hitler has visited Paris he will travel to Villiers-sur-Oise. We think he will travel there with Gottschalk and there will be a meeting of the top brass.

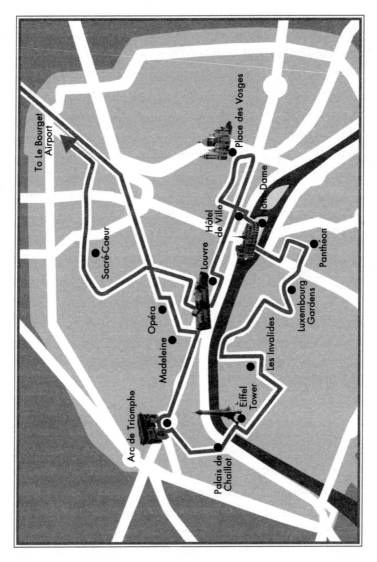

Hitler's tour of Paris, June 1940

We don't know what it's about – the future of France, maybe. We do know that there has been quite a lot of activity in that area, so it sounds like our intelligence is right. The Network we are building has different cells. There is a cell based there and it includes elements of the army from the north. If, for whatever reason, we fail tomorrow, then the cell at Villiers will have a second chance."

This time Jack raised no objections. It looked like the die was cast, and whatever his personal opinion, he and Angus were now part of the team. Finally, the long discussion came to an end and Angus nudged Jack. "We're going to get some fresh air, before it gets dark."

"OK – but don't go far. Be careful!" Jean-Yves said.

After venturing only a few metres, Jack and Angus found themselves looking out over the Seine towards the great cathedral of Notre Dame, which loomed up from the neighbouring Ile de la Cité.

"This is a complete nightmare," Jack said, finally.

"But if it wasn't for them, we'd be stuffed. I think we need to help them. They're not asking us to actually do it – just help Sophie with the signalling along the route." Angus shrugged, "Killing Hitler. Doesn't sound like a bad idea to me…"

"Get a grip, Angus. You're in VIGIL. It might seem like a good idea, but it's not. It's not meant to happen. I've never heard anything about any assassination attempt on Hitler in Paris or in this place they keep talking about – Villiers or whatever it's called."

"What do you mean?"

"I checked out the iPhone app. Take a look." Jack glanced

up and down the street to make sure they were alone and surreptitiously brought out his iPhone. He pressed a button and waved a finger across the screen. "VIGIL's historical archive app – events, places, people – the whole of history." Jack tapped in some letters. "It's even got old film footage… So I put in 'Hitler plus Paris visit plus 1940'…"

Jack tapped the screen and a grainy black-and-white film started to play.

"Recognise Paris?" Jack said. "I'll turn up the volume."

The old film was accompanied by military music and the stern voice of a German commentator. It sounded a bit tinny and they couldn't really make out the German, but they could understand the announcement of a series of famous place names: 'Opéra', 'Place de la Concorde', then, 'Trocadero'…

"A motorcade… they're German soldiers…"

"And you probably recognise that guy getting out of the front car?"

"Adolf Hitler."

"Right. I think this is an actual film of Hitler's tour of Paris, which happens tomorrow morning. It has the date and time. Back home it's probably on YouTube. Anyway, you can see the big open-top cars in the motorcade and all the sights he visits… just like Jean-Yves was saying. Basically, from this you can tell exactly where he is going and when – the information that Jean-Yves has got is pretty accurate."

The jumpy black-and-white image followed Hitler and his entourage from one Paris landmark to the next. There were also some gaps in the footage. For example, there was film of the approach to the Arc de Triomphe but then there was a gap, before the entourage was seen continuing on down Avenue Victor Hugo. The film had been extensively edited – but it was good enough.

"This film is taken *tomorrow* by the German army photographer," Angus whispered, "as Hitler tours Paris… so…"

Jack finished his sentence, "…there is nothing in there showing any kind of trouble. So either it never happens, or…"

"Or what?"

"It did happen but the Germans caught whoever did it and quietly erased the footage from history – along with everyone involved."

"You mean… like… they might erase us."

Suddenly, they were interrupted.

"What are you doing, boys?"

Jack jumped. They had been so engrossed that they had not heard Sophie come up behind them. Jack fumbled with the iPhone but was not quick enough to put it away.

"What's that?" Sophie asked, staring at the device.

"Oh, nothing, pilot stuff…"

"What? Show me."

"It's nothing, really…" Jack said anxiously.

But Sophie was insistent. "Come on – show me."

Angus said the first thing that came into his head, "Special thing you get in the RAF. Er, also plays music. Check this out. You put these plugs in your ears. It's cool." He snatched the phone from Jack's hand and offered the earplugs to Sophie.

Sophie was surprised, to say the least. Tentatively, she put the earphones in her ears and Angus tapped at the screen. Her eyes opened in amazement and slowly her lips grew into a smile. After a while, she pulled out the earplugs.

"Amazing. What did you call it? 'Cool'?"

"No that's not the name of the thing, it's just an expression, it means, er, well, I'm not sure what it means," Angus struggled. "It's just cool. Or if it's funny, it's 'LOL'. "

"LOL?"

"Er, yeah. LOL. Laugh Out Loud."

"But the music, I, it, well, it sounds so strange…"

"Yeah, er, Arcade Fire, I guess it is… They're cool too."

Angus's stunt with the iPhone was prompting Sophie to ask more and more questions.

Jack tried to take control, "Sophie, er, it's a secret thing – you know for messages, navigation and stuff – for pilots – you mustn't mention it. Never. In fact we brought it down here… because we need to get rid of it – the technology is advanced, we can't have it getting into enemy hands."

Sophie looked at the iPhone and then looked at Jack and Angus. It was if she could not quite believe what she was hearing or seeing.

Suddenly, Jack took the iPhone and threw it as far as he could out into the river.

"What are you doing?" Angus said, crossly.

Jack replied through gritted teeth, "Secret. Military. Pilot stuff. Right? Get it, Angus?"

"Can't believe you just did that…"

"Well I did – I'll explain later."

Sophie observed the sudden angry exchange between Jack and

Angus with quiet amusement. When they had finally stopped bickering she looked up at them, smiled and said, "You two are LOL."

Angus looked at her for a moment and then laughed. "Yeah. I guess we are."

The sun had already dropped below the Paris rooftops and the light was draining from the day. They gazed out across the Seine as the sky darkened. After a while, Sophie put one arm around Jack and the other around Angus.

"I am glad you will help us tomorrow. You are RAF – it is good you are here."

Jack looked into her eyes and tried to smile. "Sophie… I wish I could explain. We understand your parents' motives, but we are worried it is not going to work. I think they are endangering themselves… all of us. There are things…" he struggled to find the right words, "things you don't know, we don't know. I'm just saying I don't think it is meant to happen, it is too risky…"

But Sophie was having none of it. "My mother and father – I know they are doing the right thing. They had friends die fighting in the Battle for France. I knew some of them too. They were good people. You must help."

Jack shook his head. He was torn. He desperately wanted to help, but he had seen the future and he knew it was not meant to be. On the other hand these people, Jean-Yves, Marianne and Sophie had saved their lives and were their only real hope of survival in France. Perhaps he and Angus did not have a choice.

Jack woke with a start. His sheet was wet with sweat.

"Jack." He heard a soothing voice say his name. "It's just a dream…"

Sophie put a gentle hand on his forehead and ran her fingers through his sticky blonde hair.

"A terrible nightmare. Where am I?" Jack pushed himself up onto one elbow. The first light of dawn was just discernible at the window. He looked around the room. There were sleeping bodies lying huddled on the floor. Then he remembered. Today was the day. As Jean-Yves had said, "The day we change history."

"I think we have to get up now," Sophie whispered.

Jack could not really make out the features of Sophie's face, but he could feel her breath and smell her close to him. She stroked his forehead again. "You'll see, it will be fine. Have no regrets, *mon ami*."

Showing off on the Champs

Jack stood opposite the hulking mass of the Arc de Triomphe and peered back down the Champs-Elysées. It was six-thirty on the morning of Friday 28th June and the most famous street in the world was eerily quiet. The broad, leafy avenue fringed with elegant shops and cafés stretched endlessly before him. The only traffic was way in the distance – two low-slung black Citroëns trailing behind a convoy of canvas-covered army vehicles heading towards the Place de la Concorde. Despite the early hour, opposite him an official, wearing a black beret and with a large bucket at his feet, was painting over what looked like an evacuation plan for the city. Some of the writing could still be seen ('For the South, Itinerary 2, leaving from Porte d'Italie, for Essonnes, Fontainebleau and Nemours'). Nearby, a young bleary-eyed mother had emerged to see if the fresh morning air might quieten her children. With one hand she rocked a pram and with her other she tried to hold on to an energetic toddler who kicked dust and stones under one of the great roadside trees.

Jack found it unnerving that he knew what was about to happen. The app had showed it all. In a few minutes, a number of large, open-top, six-wheeled vehicles would drive up the Champs-Elysées towards him. In the front seat of the first car would sit Adolf Hitler – leader of the Third Reich. He would be absorbed by the grandeur of Paris and satiated by the blood of conquest. The entourage would almost completely circumnavigate the Arc de Triomphe and would then proceed directly down Avenue Victor Hugo before arriving at the Palais de Chaillot for the *Führer's* first view of the Eiffel Tower. Hitler would be inspired by his visit to Paris and, as a result, would instruct his favourite architect, Albert Speer, who was accompanying him, to resume building work in Berlin.

Except now Jack knew that, if Jean-Yves, Marianne, Ours and Patrice carried out their plan, Hitler would never see the Eiffel Tower and would not leave Paris alive.

Jack could just see Angus further down the Champs-Elysées. Angus had his head turned away from Jack and in turn was looking even further down the avenue to where Sophie would be. The three of them were spread out along the avenue, Jack at the Arc de Triomphe, Sophie about halfway down and Angus in between. As soon as Hitler's motorcade passed Sophie, she would signal to Angus, who would signal back up to Jack. Jack would then signal to Ours and Patrice, who were waiting opposite in Avenue de Friedland to make their move. Jean-Yves and Marianne waited on Avenue Foch as backup. The circular plan of grand avenues arranged around the mighty Arc de Triomphe made for a natural arena to target the motorcade and would allow an easy escape.

Although Jack could not see it, far away down the Champs-Elysées, Sophie had already spotted the *Führer's* motorcade rumbling towards her. She immediately took a red scarf and wrapped it around her neck. Angus saw the signal. He took a white cap from inside his jacket and put it on. The motorcade drove towards him. Although he was far away, Jack could clearly see the white hat on Angus's head. He waited for a few seconds, then, sure enough, he spotted the motorcade rumbling into view. Jack took a large blue handkerchief from his pocket and put it to his nose. Red, white and blue. There was no turning back now. Across the street, where Avenue de Friedland joined the Place de l'Étoile, Ours mounted his 100cc Peugeot motor scooter and revved the engine. Patrice got up behind him, riding pillion. He reached inside his leather jacket with one hand to check his revolver. In ten seconds the leading car would be moving into the Place de l'Étoile and around the Arc de Triomphe. Ours would drive his scooter right up to the side of the leading car and Patrice would fire at point-blank range at the *Führer* in the passenger seat.

Jack knew that he should do what he had been told and, having given the signal, disappear quickly to make his way back to the rendezvous. But the scene before him had a curious, hypnotic momentum. It was too much for him just to walk away. The Mercedes sedan was a great lump of a car – more like a military vehicle, and, as it moved near, Jack found himself staring, dumbfounded. It was then, finally, sitting up high in the passenger's seat that Jack saw him. The *Führer*. Adolf Hitler. He wore a dark, leather overcoat and a high, peaked army cap – like the one Gottschalk had worn at Bonaparte's. He was staring up at the great bulwark of the Arc de Triomphe, and then, for no explicable reason he lowered his gaze and looked towards Jack, standing by the road a few metres ahead. For a split second, their eyes met. Hitler's eyes were unblinking. Jack tried to understand what they communicated.

He remembered what he knew about the *Führer*. He had survived the First World War and had hacked his way through the confusion of post-war Germany to grasp control of the most powerful country in the world. Through a pernicious blend of nationalism, racism and risk taking he had harnessed an undercurrent of bitterness amongst many Germans. His bullying demands had, for many years, appeared reasonable and had been rewarded by good people inside and outside of Germany. They had the power to resist him but they were too scared to act in case they unwittingly unleashed a second war – that might be even worse than the First World War. It was only now, with nearly the whole of Europe under Nazi control, that these good people had started to understand the true horror that had been unleashed. Here was the man responsible for millions of deaths. And that was exactly what those eyes communicated – death.

Jack's trance was broken by the sound of a motorcycle engine. Almost at exactly the same time as Jack heard the engine, there was a gust of wind. It seemed odd, because the morning so far had been quite still. The wind rolled up the Champs-Elysées and dust swirled around. Jack still held his blue handkerchief limply in one hand; the wind caught it and carried it off across the street into the path of the on-coming Mercedes. It flapped and twitched in the air like a miniature kite or a pricked balloon. Nearby, the toddler spotted the flapping blue cloth. He giggled and jumped and then suddenly he broke free from his mother's hand and, to her horror, charged into the Champs-Elysées directly in front of the *Führer*'s thundering motorcade. The blue handkerchief twirled and twisted in the air and the toddler followed, his little arms outstretched to the sky, entranced and delighted by the dancing cloth.

Jack looked on aghast as the giant Mercedes zeroed in on the small child. The toddler must have heard the rumble of the engine, because he was suddenly distracted and half turned towards the on-coming car. It was at that moment Jack saw that in his little fat fingers, the boy held a small flag – a French tri-colour – and as he stared unblinking at the black bonnet of the Mercedes he gave it a little wave as if in a poignant gesture of welcome, or perhaps surrender. In five seconds he would be flattened.

The boy's mother screamed. But Jack was already in full flight. Just as the hulking vehicle slewed sideways to avoid crushing the boy, Jack appeared in front of it, reached down and, without breaking step, enveloped the boy in his arms and ran on. The Mercedes missed them by an inch. But Ours and Patrice, aboard their little Peugeot motorcycle, were not so lucky. The boy's chase across the Champs Elysées had coincided almost exactly with Ours and Patrice's interception. As the car slewed sideways to avoid Jack and the little boy, Ours and Patrice stood no chance. The wing of the car slammed into the scooter. Ours flew over the handlebars and bounced once on the bonnet before landing on the road. Patrice was thrown high and wide from his position as pillion and he too landed with a smack on the road. The Mercedes stopped and the cars in the pursuing motorcade came to a halt. Soon the whole place was swarming with German officers. The little boy held Jack's hand and observed the mayhem he had caused with bemusement. He waved his little French flag at the scene in front of him as if in some way this would magic things better. His mother appeared beside them still pushing her pram. Her face was white. She picked up the little boy and hugged him with tears streaming down her face. The little boy wriggled in her arms. Jack looked on at the melée of officers who now surrounded Ours and Patrice. What they had not yet noticed, but surely would in just a few moments, was that in the collision, something had flown free from Patrice's jacket and it now lay on the road only a few metres away. It pointed accusingly towards Patrice's prostrate body, which lay beneath the Arc de Triomphe.

A loaded revolver.

Regrattier Rendezvous

No one felt hungry. They sat round a table at the back of Berthillon's café on the Ile Saint-Louis. Jean-Yves stared into the dregs of his coffee and puffed on a Gauloise – an occasional habit and one only brought on at times of acute anxiety.

"What will they do to them?" said Sophie. It was about the twentieth time she had asked the same question.

Marianne tried to comfort her, putting an arm around her shoulder. "Stop saying that, my dear. You know Ours and Patrice… they can look after themselves." Seeking reassurance, she glanced at Jean-Yves, but he did not look up.

"They might just be taken for petty criminals – in the wrong place at the wrong time – an unfortunate accident," he said quietly. "There is no reason for the Nazis to think that they were actually trying to assassinate Hitler."

The image flashed through Jack's mind again: plucking the little boy from the on-coming Mercedes, the car slewing sideways to avoid impact and the collision with the scooter… then Ours and Patrice flat out on the road and the revolver lying there for all to see. In the mayhem, Jack, Angus and Sophie had slipped away from the scene, picked their way back to Rue le Regrattier and, thankfully, Jean-Yves and Marianne had joined them an hour later.

They had been sick with worry and had spent a sleepless night at the safe-house. Jack shivered.

"It's my fault," he said.

"No!" Marianne said. She touched his hand. "You did what we asked… against your better judgement… and you rescued that little boy. He would have died. Another innocent victim of this stupid war."

"Marianne is right," Jean-Yves said, looking up. "You were very brave, *mon ami*." He shook his head. "Perhaps we should have listened to you." He gave a little shrug. "It's almost like you knew that we were not going to succeed."

When Jean-Yves said the words, Jack felt his heart give a little jump. No one else seemed to register the comment, but, just for a moment, Jack thought that he saw Sophie looking at him with a rather odd expression from the other side of the table.

"Anyway, we can't stay in Paris any longer," Jean-Yves continued. "They will question Ours and Patrice and will already have questioned everyone at Bonaparte's. Eventually someone will talk and the Nazis will make the connection. Then they will be onto us. The whole Network is at risk, everything we have worked for."

Marianne nodded. "The longer we stay, the more dangerous it gets…"

Just as Jean-Yves took a final drag from his Gauloise, the door of the café swung open. A boy appeared from the street; he looked about ten years old. He wore shorts, a scruffy jumper and an old beret. For a moment he waited in the doorway, scanning the inside of the café. Then his eyes locked onto Marianne. He trotted over to her and removed a letter from a worn leather satchel. He put it down on the table in front of her, looked around and put a grubby index finger to his lips as if to say, 'Sshh.' Then, without saying another word, he turned and slipped quietly away.

Marianne held the letter in front of her.

Jean-Yves's eyebrows arched knowingly. "Open it, then."

Marianne unsealed the envelope and pulled out a blotchy, poorly typed piece of thin office paper. Quietly, she read out the words on the paper in a whisper and as she did so her brow furrowed.

"G has returned to VO. H with him. Celebration still planned for tonight. Join us with as many friends as you can – P."

Beneath the 'P', there was a picture of a crucifix with not one but two horizontal spars. The *Croix de Lorraine*. The symbol of the French Resistance.

Marianne took the Gauloise that smouldered at Jean-Yves lips and blew gently on its tip. Ash flickered into the air and the end of the cigarette burned a bright orange. She touched the burning cigarette to the corner of the paper and it caught fire – flaming up briefly before disintegrating in black-and-white ash.

"What does it mean, Marianne?" Jack asked.

Marianne smiled. "A message from the Network, from Pierre at Villiers. *'G has returned to VO'* – Gottschalk has returned to his headquarters in Villiers-sur-Oise. *'H with him'*. *'H'* is Hitler. It means Hitler has gone to Villiers as planned, despite what happened yesterday. *'Celebration still planned for tonight.'* It means that Pierre and his friends are still planning the attack. *'Join us with as many friends as you can.'* They want us to join them in Villiers-sur-Oise, if we can. Today."

Jean-Yves thumped the table. "It's still on. We can still get them."

The note had a transforming effect on Jean-Yves and Marianne. They were suddenly re-energised.

"We need to hurry… it will just depend on the trains," Jean-Yves said.

Marianne started to scribble on a scrap of paper. "Here Sophie, a few things to get. Meet back at the flat in thirty minutes. Then we go."

Villiers-sur-Oise

The centre of Villiers-sur-Oise was built around a shop-lined square. The church, a large stone edifice fringed with leering gargoyles, ran along the south side, throwing the war monument and a few scrubby bushes into permanent shade. The monument was a poignant composition of two soldiers in greatcoats, one fallen and the other holding aloft a billowing flag with the inscription, '*A Nos Enfants Tombés sur le Champ d'Honneur 1914-1918*'. An afternoon shower had transformed the packed earth of the deserted square into a sea of mud punctuated with cloudy, yellowish puddles and water still ran like tears down the statue.

On the north side of the square, rain dripped slowly from the faded green-and-white striped awning rolled down to protect the shop window of Mme Francette's 'La Mode Anglaise'. Rain had washed down the municipal noticeboard that shielded the public conveniences from view, staining the poster for one night only, '*Jojo Bouillon et son Orchestre*'! The rain drained through the gutter in front of the Boucherie Chevaline with its plaster horse head jutting out above the door and strings of sausages hanging in the window.

"Chez Pierre's is over there," Jean-Yves pointed at the bar-restaurant opposite, which had chairs stacked on either side of the door. They crossed the square and approached Chez Pierre. Jean-Yves tentatively pushed open the door. Inside, row upon row of gleaming glasses of all shapes and sizes stood behind the bar in a mirrored display cabinet, flanked on either side by countless bottles of alcohol, their names – Calvados, Cognac, Rivesaltes – reading like an alcoholic road map of France. Above the cabinet hung a large black-and-white photograph of an elderly moustachioed man in uniform with the caption 'Notre Maréchal'. At a high wooden cash desk to the left of the bar sat a middle-aged woman with heavily rouged lips, her hair set in a stiff swirl of complicated curls and rolls. Beside her, leaning heavily on the end of the bar, stood an elderly man with a florid face. A half-drunk glass of red wine stood by his elbow, next to an unlabelled green bottle. The man stared at the peeling, nicotine-stained Liste de Consommations on the wall, his newspaper folded and as yet unread. Except for a waiter busy laying a table, these two seemed to be the only customers in the café.

Jean-Yves went over to the waiter and murmured something in his ear. The waiter nodded towards a door. Jean-Yves led on and they found themselves in a large kitchen. Three men sitting round a table looked up as they came in. There was a hand-drawn map on the table together with two empty bottles of wine. The oldest of the men, got to his feet, smiled and shook Jean-Yves firmly by the hand.

"It is good to see you again, Pierre," Jean-Yves said.

"These are our friends from the Network – Bruno, from the village, and you know Dominic, from the Ninth army under General Corap…"

Dominic grimaced. "I was under General Corap… until we surrendered…" he took a gulp of wine, "but some of us fight on."

There followed a series of endless handshakes and additional chairs were pulled in from the restaurant so the group could gather round the table. Pierre grabbed a third bottle of wine, handed round some more glasses and pulled out the cork. Behind them, two chefs in the kitchen carried on working, chopping away obliviously. Pierre raised his glass in a toast.

"Welcome, my friends. To our success! *Courage!*"

There was an enthusiastic clashing of glasses and Pierre downed his wine in one go.

He turned to Jean-Yves. "It is wonderful that you made it here. Together, we will make history."

"We were happy to receive your message, Pierre," Marianne said. "You heard what happened to our friends Ours and Patrice? We thought perhaps the plans would change."

"Yes, we heard. It was bad luck. I hear those two are tough. They will survive. But now, yes, we will continue with our plan. For us, nothing has changed. We attack tonight. And we must explain everything so you can help us." Pierre took the wine bottle, refilled his own glass and then topped up everyone else's. The men seemed to have had quite a lot to drink already. Pierre's co-ordination was not what it might have been and the wine splashed messily as he poured.

"As you know, the Nazis have taken over the chateau two kilometres from the town – Gottschalk's headquarters when he is not in Paris. Since the surrender, activity at the chateau has increased. They are also sealing off an area in the valley below – part of the chateau woodland. They have taken over the airfield ten kilometres to the north – there is a squadron of BF109's there.

We believe all this means that the meeting with Hitler and the top brass is definitely happening."

"He is here now?" Jean-Yves asked.

Pierre's eyes widened in excitement, "Gottschalk returned to the chateau last night. We believe Hitler was with him. Everything is in place. Let me show you."

Pierre pointed to the map.

"This is Villiers-sur-Oise. That way is south – towards Paris. We are there. The airstrip is off the map in that direction. And that," he moved his finger over to a patch of woodland, "just out of town, is Chateau Villiers."

"But the chateau itself will be well protected," Jean-Yves said. "We can't just launch an attack from the outside."

Pierre smiled. "We will attack from the inside and the outside at the same time. They are taking food and supplies from the village each morning and each evening. Chez Pierre's gets daily orders. We will simply drive up in the van, delivering the provisions, and ourselves, into the building…"

"What about weapons?"

"Only explosives. Well disguised. We deliver them into the heart of the building and then leave. Simple."

"Aren't they going to be suspicious – surely they will search the van?" Marianne said.

"They are used to us, we have been supplying them for a while now. Anyway, there will only be two of us in the van. Hardly a threat. After we leave, the bomb goes off – boom!" Pierre raised his arms dramatically above his head. "And then we launch the next phase, which is where Dominic and his friends from the Ninth come in."

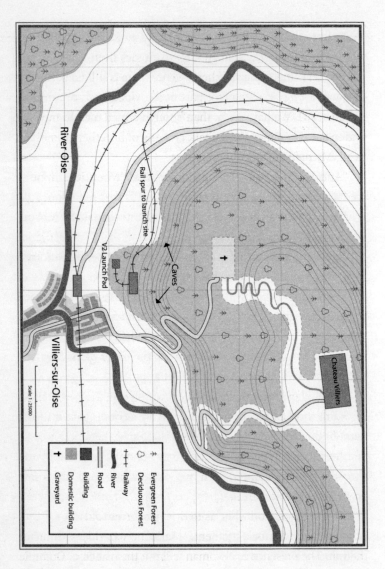

Map of the area surrounding Villiers-sur-Oise

Dominic took over. "The French army may have surrendered. But we have not. We have enough comrades from my company to launch an attack through here, where there is still no perimeter fencing," Dominic pointed at part of the woodland surrounding the chateau. "We have more than enough armed men to mop up and make sure Hitler, Gottschalk and any of his other cronies are dead. My men are already preparing."

"And we have the element of surprise. When it is done… we melt back into the countryside."

Jack glanced anxiously across the table at Angus. He was no soldier, but he knew the plan sounded very risky. The prospect of taking on an armed garrison of the SS, which was being reinforced to protect a visit from the *Führer*, with a collection of staff from Chez Pierre and the ramshackle remains of a recently defeated army, did not sound hopeful. It looked like Pierre and his friends were determined to strike when they had the chance, however, and Jean-Yves and Marianne were being carried along by their enthusiasm.

Jack looked round the table. There was steel in the eyes of these men and their confidence was buoyed by alcohol. Jack realised, with dismay, that he wouldn't to be able to stop them on his own. Not for the first time, he felt he was being dragged along by the course of events and drawn into something that he knew he should have no part in.

"So – what do you want us to do?" Jean-Yves said.

Pierre thought for a moment. "Marianne will ride with me in the van. The presence of a woman will put them at ease. Dominic will command his company through the woodlands that surround the chateau – I think you should join him." He looked up at Jack and Angus and then at Sophie. "And of course we need your help as well."

"Er, hold on…" Jack put up his hands defensively.

Pierre just talked over him. "There is a slight rise in the woodland here." He pointed at the map again. "From that position you can get a good view of the road from Villiers, the driveway from the road up to the chateau, and the chateau itself. You will be between us in the van and Dominic and his troops further along in the woods. You three should stay together. I will give you my field glasses. You just need to watch. If you see anything that worries you, run to the road to warn us or head through the woods to warn Dominic. Clear?"

Jack didn't like the sound of this at all. He cleared this throat, "But…"

Everyone looked at him and he felt the blood rushing to his face. "I am not sure – I still think maybe we should wait, er, wait until we have more people…"

Pierre looked at him, his face was flushed with excitement and the effects of the wine, "My young friend, this is the only chance we have. We must strike now. We have a second chance to kill Hitler and free France." He leaped up, swaying on his feet, "Courage, my friends…" he thrust out his glass, "for France!"

Stake-out

Pierre had described the spot well. There was a rise in the woodland and the undergrowth was sufficiently sparse to give them a reasonable view of the chateau and the surrounding area. They were about a mile from the village, up from the river that meandered through the valley below. A narrow driveway peeled off to the left of the road from Villiers through a canopy of trees which at points formed a dark and verdant tunnel, split here and there by splashes of evening sunshine. It led directly to the chateau, which sat behind closed bottle green, wrought-iron gates. There were sentries posted both at the main gates and at the entrance where the drive split from the road.

The chateau itself was a well-proportioned rectangular structure. It was two storeys high, with a rounded tower at each end and a sharply sloping slate roof. Solid double doors were flanked on either side by large windows, eight on the ground floor in all and nine on the first floor. The roof was set with a series of bull's-eye windows. At the front, the gravel drive leading from the gates widened into a broad 'T', and ended abruptly at the left gable but continuing off from the right end to a low block of outbuildings and stables. The rim of grass around the chateau was neatly trimmed and after thirty metres merged into the woodland.

Jack had found a good position up in an old oak tree. Angus and Sophie lay in a large bush beneath it. He looked out towards the woods beyond the far end of the chateau. He knew that in there, somewhere, Dominic and his company of men would be waiting, poised to attack. Looking back towards the chateau, he spotted a young deer nibbling on a tuft of grass at the edge of the lawn. Jack raised his field glasses and surveyed each of the windows. He half expected to spot the *Führer* gazing out at him, but he couldn't see anyone inside the building. At the entrance, two soldiers stood guard. On the roof, two more soldiers chatted. One was smoking and puffed smoke rings up into the still evening air.

"I can hear something on the road!" Angus whispered up from his hiding position.

Jack's heart jumped. Sure enough, from the road below, he could hear the rough engine of the little Citroën van as it chugged its way up the gentle gradient from Villiers-sur-Oise. Jack turned his field glasses to the road. Between the trees he caught glimpses of the van and the worn red lettering on its side that spelled out, 'Chez Pierre'. From his position it was impossible to see the driver and passenger, but he knew Marianne and Pierre were in the van. Jack heard the sound of the engine drop as they reached the first checkpoint where the driveway to the chateau led off from the main village road. Jack held his breath. The engine started up again as it was allowed on its way up to the second checkpoint, at the large wrought-iron gates at the far end of the driveway.

The van stopped in front of the gates. Using his field glasses, Jack could clearly see the German sentry poke his head into the van. He walked around the van and looked under it and then returned to the cabin. Jack saw Pierre get out of the cabin and go to the back of the van. He opened the back and the sentry peered in. A second sentry stood back, one hand on his machine gun, which hung loosely by its strap from his shoulder. The rear of the van was stacked high with boxes – wine, vegetables and meat. The sentry looked at the mountain of provisions and gave a little shrug. He wasn't seriously expected to search through all of it was he? Pierre looked at the soldier expectantly and then the soldier said something. Pierre pulled down the cover at the back of the van and climbed back into the cabin. The sentry leaned into the cabin again and pointed towards the back of the chateau. The gates creaked open and the sentry smacked the side of the van twice with his hand. The van rumbled slowly through the gate and followed the driveway round to the rear of the chateau. They were in.

Jack's heart was beating even faster now and the field glasses were becoming damp with the sweat from his hands. He brought the glasses to bear once more on the front of the chateau. Firstly, he looked at the rooftop. The two German soldiers who had been there a moment ago had disappeared. The soldiers had also disappeared from the front terrace. Jack scanned the front of the building to see where they had gone. At the edge of the woods the deer was still there. But, suddenly, it lifted its head and its ears pricked up. Then it darted into the safety of the woods.

Something was wrong.

Jack kept his eye on the edge of the woods and glanced at his watch. Ten minutes to eight. Any minute now, the van should reappear… and just after eight o'clock there would be a massive explosion as the bomb ripped through the building. Then, Dominic and his company of men would break from the woods in an all-out attack on the chateau as any survivors tried to flee the building. He looked at his watch again and then over to the edge of the woods. He glanced down at Angus in the bush below. Angus frowned and mouthed a silent, "Where are they?" in return. Two more minutes passed. Still nothing. Jack looked through the field glasses again, desperately scanning the chateau, gardens and woods for any sign of life.

Suddenly, he heard a twig snap behind him. He twisted round and the shock of what he saw sent a pulse through his body. Below and about fifty metres behind, a line of German soldiers were creeping slowly through the woods. They were spread out at about ten-metre intervals, among the trees in a long line that stretched as far as Jack could see to the left and the right. They moved forward slowly, guns at the ready. One of them was approaching the thicket beneath Jack, where Angus and Sophie lay, covered in the undergrowth. Jack wanted to scream out to them to run, but he knew to do so would mean instant death. His heart was thumping in his chest like a steam hammer but he tried to stay still. He wanted the great oak tree somehow to absorb him into its vast, ancient boughs. He knew that any disturbance, any movement, would give him away. The soldiers continued to advance – maintaining a disciplined formation as best they could over the terrain. As Jack peered towards them, he suddenly noticed that after the first line of soldiers came a second wave – only twenty metres behind. The entire woodland was infested.

Jack spied the soldier nearest to them. He was only a few metres away now and Jack could clearly make out his face. Suddenly, he stopped right under the tree where Jack was hiding. He looked surreptitiously left, and then right. He undid his trousers and started to urinate on the tree. Angus and Sophie lay in the thicket next to the tree only feet away. He zipped himself up and moved off as the first line of troops eased past them. Jack looked out towards the road to their right and to the fields in the far distance beyond the outbuildings. It was difficult to see properly, but everywhere he looked he saw German soldiers approaching the chateau. The entire chateau and its grounds were surrounded by two vast contracting rings of German soldiers.

Jack looked on aghast. Emerging from the woodland on the far side of the gardens he saw a straggling band of men in civilian clothes. They had their arms held high above their heads. Behind them, German soldiers, toting machine guns, pushed them forward. In front, Jack could see Jean-Yves and Dominic, ashen-faced and terrified. They had been pulled to one side and there was a brief exchange with a Nazi officer. Then the remaining men were lined up, facing the low wall at the front of the chateau, as the two lines of soldiers, which had now passed by Jack, Angus and Sophie, emerged from the woodland and onto the chateau lawn.

Jack scrambled down from his tree and pulled Angus and Sophie up from their hiding place in the undergrowth.

"They've caught them. It's like they knew there was going to be an attack. Look…" Jack pointed through the trees to where they could see a number of the men being lined up against the wall. Sophie and Angus peered forward to where Jack pointed. Sophie started sobbing, "Can you see Mum and Dad?"

Jack grimaced, "I think I saw your dad, Sophie. Your mum was in the van, of course, but it hasn't reappeared."

Jack put the field glasses back up to his eyes. It was much more difficult to see from ground level than from his vantage point up in the big oak tree. The German soldiers now stepped away from the men lined up against the wall, forming a semi-circle around the prisoners.

"Hold on, they're not going to…" They looked on at the scene in the garden before them and then Sophie turned to Jack in bewilderment.

"Oh God, no…" Jack looked away just as the sound of automatic rifle fire ripped through the evening air. It reverberated through the woodland until there was silence. When Jack looked back up all he could see was blood spattered across the garden wall and a heap of bodies lying on the ground beneath. Sophie turned to Jack and Angus and screamed. It was not a human scream.

She burst forward, but Angus grabbed her arm. She tore at him with her nails and lashed out with her feet, screaming hysterically, but Angus held her tight. He looked over at Jack with horror in his eyes and shook his head. The screams alerted the German soldiers who turned to search out the source of the noise. Jack saw an officer bark an order and point. They had been spotted.

"Run!" Jack shouted.

Manhunt

They pelted through the woodland away from the chateau. Jack heard the muffled shouting of the soldiers through the trees behind them.

"Down here!" Angus had found a narrow woodland path – much easier going than the undergrowth – and they sprinted onwards. The path led into a clearing in the woodland. Directly ahead, there was a rusting iron gate set between high walls which extended across the clearing. They peered through. Inside, they could see rows of old graves intertwined with gravel paths. The graveyard walls were lined with cypress trees; their arrowheads pierced the evening sky.

"Come on!" Angus whispered. The gate creaked as he pushed it open. They squeezed through and Jack scraped the iron bolt back into place.

"I think that's the main gate on the other side. There must be a track that leads back to the village."

They raced across the graveyard. The path twisted under an old yew tree near the centre and for a moment they found themselves in near darkness. As they emerged, Jack's eye was drawn to an elaborate mausoleum in a far corner of the cemetery, surrounded by more yew trees. He heard voices nearby in the woods again. The soldiers were getting nearer.

"I think we've had it, Jack. I don't think we'll make it to the village," Angus said.

"Maybe we could hide in there?"

"That temple thing – you're kidding?"

They moved closer. Beside the tomb, a statue of the Virgin Mary reached out her arms, as if in welcome. Light from a few votive candles flickered and danced over her face.

Jack looked into the mausoleum. Its entrance was shielded with a low gate and a number of large vases placed on the stone floor. Behind the gate there was just an empty black space, leading down to the crypt.

"Wait here…" Jack said.

He raced off, leaving Angus and Sophie standing by the mausoleum. He ran down the gravel path towards the main gate of the graveyard. Again, he heard the soldiers' voices. The main gate was larger than the gate they had come through at the back of the graveyard. As gently as he could, he scraped the bolt to the side. Then he pushed one of the large gates so that it was partially ajar. It might just be enough to persuade their pursuers that they had run straight through the graveyard, out the other side and on to Villiers-sur-Oise in the valley beyond.

Jack retraced his steps to where Angus and Sophie still stood.

"Let's go," he whispered.

Taking one of the candles from the statue, he gingerly approached the mausoleum. He picked his way through the vases on the floor and then pushed on the metal gate. It was open. Angus and Sophie followed.

"I don't like this," Angus said.

"Sshh!" Jack whispered.

The candle gave just enough light to show the way down

a narrow stone staircase that descended into the crypt. The atmosphere changed immediately – it was cold and musty. As they reached the floor of the crypt, Jack held up the candle. Ahead of them two large stone tombs were raised on a plinth. It was difficult to see, but all around the chamber there were recesses built into the walls. Lying in each of them were coffins.

"This is too creepy."

"Keep your voice down, we need to hide somewhere, I thought the crypt would be bigger than this."

Jack moved over to one of the recesses and half tugged at the side of the coffin. It did not move.

"What are you doing? Hold on – there's no way I'm getting in…"

"No – you're right."

"What about this?"

Sophie had moved over to the far side of the crypt and was crouching down. "I think there is air here – a little breeze – and the wall here, it's not stone, it's wood. It smells rotten."

Jack and Angus moved over to Sophie. The candle was burning low and Jack held it close to the wall. The light flickered briefly onto Sophie's face. She looked as scared as Jack felt. He could see her eyes were still red from crying and the grazes on her face where the branches had clawed at her as she broke free from their hiding place.

Jack touched the door. "You're right – wood."

"And what's that?" Angus rubbed his finger round an indentation half way up. "A keyhole. It's an old door. Leave this one to me."

Without warning, he dropped his shoulder and charged the

door. It fractured and flew inwards off the remains of its hinges. Angus had not expected it to come free quite so easily. He was propelled into a passageway beyond, landing face down in mud and slime.

"You OK?" Jack called into the darkness.

"Got dirt in my face. Bring that candle over."

Angus pulled himself up from the ground.

"What is this place?"

Jack held the candle to the wall of the passageway. By its light they could just make out a narrow passage stretching out into the darkness. Jack moved his face closer to the side wall and then nearly jumped out of his skin. His stare was returned by the hollow eyes of a human skull that rested in one of a series of recesses built into the wall.

"That's sick," Angus said, staring at the skull.

"I think it's some sort of old tomb or catacomb. This graveyard must be built on an older graveyard," Sophie said.

"So if we follow this passage – it might lead somewhere?" Jack said.

"You want to go in even further?" Angus said.

"We've no choice. Let's go."

They crept on. Jack did not know whether it was better or worse to have the candle. With its meagre light he could just make out the grim shapes and shadows of human bones and skulls. Without it, they would have been spared the sight, but they would have had to feel their way, with the dreadful knowledge that at some point they might inadvertently touch something horrible. After a while there were no more recesses and the old man-made stone wall ended and gave way to natural rock which seemed quite light in colour.

"Stop!" Angus said.

Abruptly, the walls of the passageway on either side disappeared altogether and directly ahead of them there was only a huge, black, empty space. Jack held the candle above his head to see if its faint light might pick out any structure or shape in the darkness before them. Gradually, as their eyes adjusted, they started to discern a series of large ghostly shapes in the darkness ahead. Hanging in mid-air, there were a number of elongated spikes of grey–white rock that tapered downwards like giant icicles.

"Careful!" Angus pointed down. They had edged closer to a lip of rock beyond which there was no discernible floor. The passageway had led them to a high shelf above a cliff which opened into some sort of vast underground cavern.

"Caves," Jack said. "Limestone caves. I think those are stalactites – big ones."

"Over here," Sophie said. She pointed down. "It's a ladder or something."

An old metal ladder was screwed into the side of the cliff face. It led down from the rock shelf into the depths of the cave.

"Looks like no one's been here for a while," said Angus. "Shall I try it? If it goes down into the bottom of the cave… maybe it leads somewhere… maybe it'll lead us out." Angus grabbed the top of the ladder and shook it.

"It's a bit knackered – but seems secure. Here goes…"

He slid himself over the lip and put his feet on a metal rung. Jack and Sophie peered down and watched as the top of Angus's head disappeared into the gloom below. Soon he was out of sight.

A moment later, they heard him call up. "I'm down. It's not far. Come on."

In a couple of minutes they were all at the bottom of the cave.

"Stalagmites too… it's incredible."

"Never mind that," Angus said. "Is there a way through?"

"There," Jack pointed. It's definitely some sort of path."

They set off again, picking their way through the swirling shapes and spikes of the limestone rock formations.

"The cave seems to taper in there."

Gradually, the cavern narrowed and they clambered through a sequence of smaller caves and chambers. They rounded a corner and, in front of them, a wall rose from the ground right up to the ceiling.

"Blocked."

Jack reached out and touched the wall.

"But it's wood. Planking. It's been put there. The cave has been sealed off. There must be something on the other side."

"Do you think we can knock it down?" Angus said.

"We don't want to make a noise. We've no idea what's on the other side."

They started to run their hands over the wooden planks; checking for any gaps or weaknesses.

"You know, I think it looks quite new… the wood smells fresh."

"And put up in a hurry – over here – there is a loose plank," Sophie said, beckoning them towards her.

Angus wobbled the plank. "It's only nailed at one end. If I push…"

He eased his weight against the plank which bent inwards, creating a hole big enough to step through. He released the plank and it snapped shut again. Angus was on the other side.

"What's there?" Jack whispered.

"Can't really see. The passage goes on for a bit, but it's quiet, I'll hold the plank open and you guys can squeeze through."

Soon Jack and Sophie were on the other side too. Gingerly, they crept forward along the passage. The candle flickered and Jack felt the air around them warming.

"I think we must be near the entrance."

Gradually the passageway began to open out into a low cave. Ahead, a series of rectangular shapes loomed into view. As they moved closer they saw that the shapes were huge wooden crates.

"Someone's using the cave for storage."

"It can't be far to another entrance."

They squeezed through the narrow space between the cave wall and the line of crates. Occasionally, they stopped to listen. But the makeshift warehouse seemed completely bereft of life. Finally, they reached the end and Jack peered round the last of the crates. In the darkness, he didn't notice the lettering stamped on the side of each crate. Even if he had seen the words, he would not have been able to understand them, because they were in German. However, he would have recognised the bold black symbol printed next to the words. A Nazi swastika. In front of the crates, there was just an empty space. Jack took the lead now, waving the others forward.

"No one here. And I think we can get through here."

They rushed forward to a small door that was set into huge wooden gates that filled the entrance to the cave.

"It's open," Jack said, trying the handle.

They stepped through the door and Jack sucked in the sweet night air. They were free.

There was enough light for them to work out that they were in some sort of clearing, but still in the middle of woodland. In the distance, to their left, they could make out a line of outbuildings. There was light coming from the buildings and they could hear voices and the hum of a generator.

"Not that way – I can hear people…" Jack said.

"There's some kind of mini railway track built into the ground, just here," Angus said.

"We need to get out of this clearing. I think we should go across and then into the woods. I don't know what this place is, but I'm guessing we shouldn't be here. And we still can't be all that far from the chateau."

They started to make their way across the clearing, but had only managed twenty paces when suddenly, out of nowhere, two army jeeps appeared. They were caught directly in the powerful beam of the headlights. Jack's heart sank. He tried to see who was in the jeep but the lights were blindingly bright. He heard footsteps as a man approached and then stopped right in front of them. Jack squinted, but he could not make out the face. The man spoke and Jack thought he recognised the voice.

"How nice to see you again," he said.

A Fireside Chat

The Death's Head leered at Jack. It was as if the Nazi emblem, with its grinning teeth, was mocking him from its position at the centre of the officer's cap. It was the same man, for sure: the trim uniform, the iron cross at his throat and, on his right collar, the identical zigzags side by side like lightning bolts. Jack recognised the thin, anaemic face set in a head that seemed a little too small for the cap and he recognised the eyes. They were an intense green colour.

Axel Gottschalk stared at him. Jack half-expected that, if he blinked, the man's eyes would close not from above – like a human eye – but from the side, like some as yet undiscovered Amazonian lizard waiting to devour its prey. But the face had changed since Jack had last seen it. The bridge of the nose was covered with a plaster and on one cheek a second plaster oozed blood from the wound beneath. The skin around the jaw line and extending to the mouth was raw and weeping. Jack clearly remembered Antoine screwing the glass of flaming brandy into his face. He remembered Antoine's brief expression of joy and then the terrible consequence of his act of defiance, and shuddered.

"Time for some answers." Gottschalk spoke English with only a slight accent. It was a drab monotone betraying no emotion.

They sat in a drawing room which stretched all the way from the front of Chateau Villiers to the back. Sunlight flooded through the windows onto the room's dark wood panelling. It was topped with blue wallpaper, which showed a pastoral vignette of a couple picnicking by a lake, repeated again and again. The innocence of the scene contrasted with the fear in the pit of Jack's stomach. Gottschalk sat in a high-backed armchair in front of the fireplace and peered at Jack, who sat on one of three sofas grouped around a low coffee table that was cluttered with a heavy crystal ashtray, a humidor packed with cigars and several newspapers. But Jack's eye was drawn to something else that looked oddly out of place on the coffee table. It was a crude model of a ship. A battleship with some lettering on the side, which Jack could not read. It looked like a child's toy.

"First, trouble in Paris… and now here." Gottschalk dabbed at the raw skin on his cheek with a white handkerchief.

It was several hours since they had broken free from the underground catacomb, only to be caught trying to escape from the clearing into the woods. Since then they'd endured the best part of a sleepless night in the dark, in one of the cellars beneath the chateau, terrified of what might happen to them. Then Jack had been dragged out on his own, leaving Angus and Sophie behind. It looked like they were to be interrogated separately. Jack glanced at the intricately carved mantelpiece, which showed a bloody hunting scene with snarling dogs and a cornered fox about to be ripped limb from limb. He understood how the fox must have felt.

Gottschalk continued, "Your friends in Paris were kind enough to give us the identities of all your collaborators. Initially they were reluctant of course, but after *treatment*, they were more than generous with their information: names, places… this so-called 'Network' of resistors… and this mad plan to kill the *Führer*, first in Paris and now here. As soon as we found out we laid our trap. We arranged for the *Führer* to return safely to Berlin but pretended he was still coming here. I briefed him when we were together in Paris. I will shortly have the pleasure of reporting to him that, not only have we broken a dangerous French resistance group, but we have executed our plan and added the British Empire to our list of conquests."

Jack had no idea what Gottschalk was talking about. He wanted to run, but sentries stood at each of the doors, silently watchful and more guards were posted out on the terrace. This time, escape was impossible.

"You're a murderer," Jack spat. "We saw you machine gun those men – you already had them prisoner."

Gottschalk eyed Jack with curiosity rather than annoyance. His dull monotone did not change. "May I remind you that we are at war and all our actions are entirely justified."

"I thought you had signed a peace…" Jack said.

Gottschalk shrugged. "In any conflict, there will be a period when unpleasant things have to be done until stability can be restored. Competition, conflict, death, renewal – it's our nature – we might as well accept it. If we do, things become more… simple."

"Why haven't you killed us, then?" Jack blurted out.

Again the same monotone, "You, my friend, are… interesting. A complication. In fact, you worry me. It seems that this Network is not just confined to some hotheads here in Paris and the north of France. Your presence, and that of your friend, would seem to indicate a British connection. This is concerning. Particularly given that our time is drawing close."

"What time? What is drawing close?"

Gottschalk got up and walked to a large, parchment-coloured globe on a pedestal, with its top pulled back to reveal a selection of bottles and decanters. He poured himself a drink, took a sip and put the glass down.

He moved closer until his face was only an inch from Jack's. Now his demeanour changed and it became more threatening. "That's not your concern, my friend. But the British are my concern. You are English. You are part of the Network and therefore you must be able to tell us."

"What?"

"What is the British connection with the Network and what do they know of Villiers?"

"I don't know…" Jack stuttered. "We're just caught up in this by mistake…"

Gottschalk paused, collected himself and said venomously, "You were at Bonaparte's café in Paris, you are linked to the hotheads here and you are British. We want to know exactly who you are. We know there is a British connection. I think you are a spy. God knows why they are using people so young… either they are desperate or they must assume you will be above suspicion."

Jack looked back at Gottschalk defiantly. Even if he wanted to tell the truth, there was no way Gottschalk would ever believe him.

"Very well. I am giving you one hour to think about your

response. If you refuse to speak during that time – well – I think you know what happens next."

He clapped his hands. Suddenly, two of the guards marched over. They pulled Jack to his feet.

"Take him back downstairs. Double the guard detail around the site. The time is getting close and we don't want any more… interruptions. Bring the girl up next, we will try her." He pondered for a moment. "We are running out of time. We should plan harsher measures…"

"Sir?" the guard asked.

"Yes – plan to assemble the remaining prisoners in an hour and warn the airfield."

Jack was taken from the room.

Gottschalk was alone. He moved over to the coffee table, reached down and picked up the small wooden battleship. He inspected it closely. The crude matchstick guns, turrets and masts had fallen off long ago. The toy ship was dirty and old. It should probably have been thrown away many years before. But Gottschalk cradled it carefully in his hand and inspected it closely from all angles. On the bow of the ship, crudely etched in ink with a school boy's hand were the words 'SMS *König*'. Gottschalk ran his finger over the lettering. For a moment he was transported somewhere far away: a spring morning a long time ago, a pretty wood where a young boy raced a toy ship down a bubbling stream. Gottschalk's eyes moistened, although anyone watching would not have noticed. He blinked suddenly, put the model ship down and moved over to the globe. He closed the lid and drew his finger gently over the map of Europe from Berlin to Paris. His finger stopped there for a moment and then it traced a line across the English Channel to London, then across the Atlantic to New York. He swivelled the globe gently and it came to rest again at Moscow. He closed his eyes, and for the first time in a while, a smile shaped his lips. He had waited a long, long time. But finally his Day of Vengeance was coming.

Jack was marched through the corridors of the chateau and then down the spiral staircase to the cellars. A soldier opened a wooden cellar door and pushed him inside.

Sophie jumped up from a mattress on the floor and threw her arms around him. "I thought they were going to kill you..."

Jack was surprised, but the warmth of Sophie's arms around him brought a rush of comfort. He felt a lump in his throat.

"Did they say anything about Mum and Dad?"

Jack shook his head, "Sorry Sophie... I don't know."

"You!" The guard grabbed Sophie by the shoulder and hauled her from the cellar. "Your turn to meet the boss. Come on..."

Jack caught the terror in Sophie's eyes and reached out to her. But before he could say anything more, she was gone and the door was slammed shut and locked.

"Jack – you're OK. Thank God," Angus said. "Did they do anything to you?"

"No... it was just Gottschalk." Jack shook his head. "I don't know what we're going to do, Angus, he thinks we're British Intelligence or something... wants to know how we're connected to the Network."

"But we don't know anything."

"That's the problem. I'm really scared, Angus, I think if he doesn't get what he wants soon, well, I don't know what's going to happen... but it's not good."

Jack slumped to the floor and put his head in his hands. Angus sat down beside him and stared blankly at the wall opposite.

After a while, the key turned in the lock of the door again.

"I guess Gottschalk's finished with Sophie," Angus said, looking up.

The door swung open, but it was not Sophie who was pushed into the cellar. It was a man. Someone Jack and Angus knew well. Very well indeed.

It was Dr Pendelshape.

Gottschalk's Plan

Pendelshape had lost weight. He was thinner and the lines on his forehead had become more accentuated with stress and fatigue. His deep-set eyes had dark bags under them and his grey hair, usually closely cropped and neat, had grown dishevelled and wispy. The plumpness in his face had gone and his cheeks had hollowed out. He sat opposite Jack and Angus in the cellar with his arms clasped around his knees. He looked tired and old and seemed to be ageing still further with the barrage of questions he was enduring from the two boys. They had already pumped him for information on his miraculous escape from the Armada in 1588, the attack on VIGIL and his mission to 1940. Pendelshape was stunned to discover Jack and Angus had escaped the Revisionist assault and had even witnessed his kidnapping in London.

"What about Gottschalk?" Angus asked. "What do you know about him?"

Pendelshape snorted disdainfully, "One of the worst. An ambitious Nazi, drunk on military success and power. A rising star. Known to the *Führer* personally. In fact, I think he might want to *be* the *Führer*." Pendelshape put his head in his hands. His shoulders started to shake. "I have been an idiot. It's all gone wrong. A disaster. A nightmare."

"You need to tell us everything – from the beginning," Jack said.

Pendelshape dropped his hands into his lap and stared blankly at the floor as he spoke.

"The Second World War was the worst disaster in human history. We could stop it in its tracks. Millions of lives would be saved and we could guide a democratic coalition of nations to rapid global dominance. Our plan was to go to the British government and offer them modern technology that would give them an unassailable military advantage."

"What do you mean?"

Pendelshape looked at him guiltily. "We needed something that would defeat Nazi Germany. We modelled a number of scenarios before we selected the preferred one. But we knew it was no good trying to intervene in history if VIGIL could stop us. We had to destroy VIGIL once and for all to make our plans stick. We had thought about it before, of course, but VIGIL security is too good…"

Jack felt anger welling up inside him. "Unless you have help on the inside… right?"

"Yes – we managed to turn Belstaff and Johnstone… and with them on board, the assault on VIGIL finally became possible."

"You realise that your thugs nearly killed us? When we left, it wasn't looking great for the others," Jack said angrily.

Angus jumped to his feet and bellowed into Pendelshape's face, "YOU ARE NOT MUCH BETTER THAN THAT NUTCASE UPSTAIRS!"

Pendelshape curled up in fear. Jack pulled Angus back.

"I know you can't understand… but nothing is more important than our work… we can change history… change the world."

"Just tell us what you did."

"When I got the signal from Johnstone and Belstaff that VIGIL would be under our control, I started on the next phase of the plan. I travelled back to England in early 1940. Using our research, I made an initial contact. He was a physicist based in Cambridge. He was called Petersen – he met all the criteria. He could help me. Slowly I gained his confidence, showed him blueprints and plans and we started to work together to prepare our approach to the British government. But then something happened."

"Your kidnap in London?"

"No Jack, something else. Something before that…"

"What?" Jack said.

Pendelshape sighed. "You don't know, do you?"

"Know what?"

"It's your father, Jack, he's here in 1940."

The words hit Jack like a blow from a sledgehammer. "What?"

"Yes. In fact I think he's in France. I just hope to God he's still alive."

"But…" Jack was confused yet excited at the same time.

"Let me try to explain. After I had been in London for a while, your father turned up. Out of the blue. I was shocked to say the least… and we had, er, an extremely tricky conversation. He was angry. Very angry. Anyway, he had infiltrated the Revisionist base – he knows all the systems well, of course, but still, I think he must have been helped. I should have known better, taken better precautions, but I suppose I was too eager. I was finally free to implement our plans, I didn't imagine that…."

"Get on with it…"

"Right. Well, your father had been watching me for a while in 1940 and finally he confronted me in London. He had devastating news. He claimed my contact in Cambridge, Petersen, had betrayed me. The Nazis were blackmailing him. Your father said that Petersen had passed all my blueprints over to them. I was mortified. We hadn't even started our approach to the British government." Pendelshape's breathing quickened. It was as if he were about to have some sort of panic attack.

"Get a grip."

"I'm trying," Pendelshape paused and took three slow, deep breaths. "Your father and I had to work out how far the Nazis had taken my plans and how we could undo the damage. I stayed in London, keeping a low profile, and your father travelled to the continent. He took a risk, but it was necessary. I got a message from him to say that the Nazis had made startling progress. Gottschalk had been put in charge of their operation. His ruthlessness made him ideal. Your father said he was going to try and stop them."

"I don't get it – what are you talking about – these blueprints that the Nazis stole from you… what are they?" Angus asked.

Pendelshape squirmed, reluctant to say any more.

"Spit it out," Angus said.

"The Revisionist plan was to deliver to the British government a weapon and a delivery system to go with it. To you, that means a rocket. We have detailed blueprints and plans – all based on materials that can be sourced in 1940. It would give the allies an unassailable military advantage. The war would be over. You've heard of the V-2 rocket?"

"Hold on, you are saying that the Nazis, led by Gottschalk, have copies of your blueprints to build a rocket – a V-2 rocket – and they have had these plans for months?"

"Yes."

"But you said two things. A 'delivery system' – that's the rocket – but also you said 'weapon'. You need a weapon to go in the rocket. What do you mean? What is the weapon?"

Pendelshape grimaced. "I…"

"Tell us!" Angus hissed. *What is the weapon?*"

Pendelshape said the words quickly and quietly as if hoping they might not be heard, "A nuclear weapon."

"What?" Jack was stunned.

"A nuclear dirty bomb. Not anything like the Hiroshima bomb. That would be too sophisticated. Our weapon is lower tech – one that can be built more easily in 1940. Sand impregnated with a cocktail of radioactive materials and a dispersion device, but in many ways just as devastating as a real nuclear weapon. It could render a city uninhabitable for years. One demonstration of its capabilities would end the war."

"But, how on earth would you create that kind of thing… you need a nuclear reactor or something, don't you?" Jack said.

Pendelshape shrugged. "It's not hard if you know how."

"So, let me get this right. The Nazis, led by Gottschalk, have plans that tell them how to build a V-2 rocket and to create radioactive material to go inside it. And they have had these plans for months. And now they have you." Jack's voice rose an octave, "You thought you had it all worked out, didn't you? You thought you could change the world… and now look what you've done.

You've got a madman running around with a rocket and an actual *nuclear bomb* – only trouble is… he's on the WRONG SIDE!"

Something inside of Jack snapped. He rushed forward, bunched his fist and smashed it into Pendelshape's face. He would have landed a second punch but Angus just caught him. Blood oozed from Pendelshape's nose and he held his hand up to his face.

"Enough…" Angus held Jack in a vice-like grip. "But you deserved that, I've a good mind to finish you off."

Pendelshape held his head in his hands and as they stared at him accusingly, his shoulders suddenly started to shake. He sobbed and tears poured down his face, mingling with the blood from his nose until his shirt was wet and pink. Between the sobs they caught an occasional word, "We… are… trying to… do… good… trying… to save mankind… from itself…"

Jack eased himself from Angus's grip. He'd felt a strange sense of release by lashing out at Pendelshape. Perhaps it had been a long time coming. But now, looking at him sobbing in a heap, the man with the great intellect and driving, warped ambition to change the world, didn't look so great. In fact, he looked pathetic.

"The British government, what about them?"

"They don't know anything. I agreed with your father that I would do nothing and say nothing until we understood how far the Nazis had got with my plans. Only then could we determine the intervention we needed to reverse the situation. Your father took my time phone and all my original plans and blueprints. In the meantime, I kept up a pretence with Petersen. But I think he was getting nervous about staying in England. Somehow the newspapers had got onto something, they knew the government was searching for ideas and Petersen is quite a well-known scientist; they must have guessed that the government would probably consult him. There was even an article where some journalist had spotted Petersen with me. Gottschalk finally decided that it was too risky to leave us both in London. That's why they kidnapped me. They've got Petersen now as well."

Somewhere from up in the chateau they could here muffled voices.

Jack cocked his ear to the ceiling. "I don't know how we get out of this. Gottschalk gave me an hour to come up with something and that's nearly up."

Jack tried to assimilate all he had learned from Pendelshape. The Revisionists were out of control. They had got rid of his father – clearly the only person who could give them the leadership they needed. They had hatched a new plan – a new intervention in history. This time it was even more dangerous than before – taking back detailed plans for a rocket and a nuclear weapon to a continent already at war. It was madness. A nuclear weapon under the control of Hitler and the Nazis did not bear thinking about, but the Revisionists had delivered one right into their hands.

"One last thing," Jack said. "Why are they all here – you know, Gottschalk, the military garrison... what's special about this place?"

Pendelshape shrugged. "Obviously it must be near here..."

"What's near here?"

"The launch site of course... for the rocket."

"Of course. That explains all the activity. Hitler was coming here to visit the site. Maybe even to watch the launch. And that cave with all the equipment and the clearing with the outhouses... it's all part of it. No wonder Gottschalk is so paranoid."

There was a moment of silence as they pondered this. Finally, Angus said, "Your dad's, still out there, Jack, he knows about the plans – the rocket and the bomb. He knows he must stop it and so he must know about this place. He must know about Villiers."

Jack nodded. "Yes, you're right. He's our only hope. If he's still alive."

Time was running out. Despite everything that Pendelshape had told them, there was only one thing on Jack's mind. He knew that he was supposed to tell Gottschalk all about the British involvement with the Network and what they knew about Villiers. He had already seen what Gottschalk did to people who did not do what he wanted. They would be his next victims. Jack clung on to one hope. It was a tiny speck of light in the darkness. It was the strange image that he had seen from the Taurus – of himself and the person he was sure must be his father, standing next to him. As the days had gone on and their nightmare had worsened, the memory had started to crumble. Jack was beginning to doubt he had seen anything at all. But Pendelshape had told him that his father was back in 1940. In fact he was *here* – in France – perhaps even near Villiers. With that revelation, the memory had suddenly appeared in his mind as clear as day. He didn't want to talk about it, because he still did not know what it really meant. But he clung onto it, because it was the only hope he had.

They heard a key in the door to the cellar and it creaked open. A soldier stood in the doorway. Sophie was standing just behind, guarded by more soldiers. Her eyes were red and she looked very scared.

"Your time is up," the soldier said. "You will all come with us."

A Good German

They stepped down from the back of the army truck. Jack reckoned they must have been inside it for about an hour, but he had soon lost any sense of time or direction as they jiggled their way from the chateau. He blinked in the sunlight. The land in front of them was flat, surrounded on three sides by low woodland, which stood tall behind a high perimeter fence. They had parked up beside an aircraft hangar and, nearby, Jack counted five military aircraft. In the distance were some outbuildings and Jack saw a strip of concrete leading off into the far distance – a runway. He remembered what Pierre had told them about an airfield to the north of Villiers. Maybe this was it.

Parked outside the aircraft hangar was an army truck and two, six-wheeled armoured vehicles. There were also a couple of smaller, open-topped, army jeeps with spare tyres attached to the peculiarly angled front bonnets. There was a sudden roar as two BF109s flew low over the airfield before banking sharply in the distance. The German army and the Luftwaffe were here in force. Whatever was inside the hangar, it was important.

Jack saw a plume of dust kick into the air as two low-slung, black civilian cars emerged through the main entrance to the airstrip. They drew up next to the hangar. An SS soldier saluted, held open the passenger door on one side of the car and Gottschalk stepped out. He waited for the second car to pull up.

A man in civilian clothing got out. He was slim and wore a light suit and a dark tie. Gottschalk moved over to him and saluted. The man ignored the salute and just nodded in return. Gottschalk gestured towards the giant hangar. As they moved closer to where Pendelshape, Jack, Angus and Sophie stood, Jack suddenly recognised the civilian. It was the man they had seen enter Bonaparte's café just before Gottschalk had shot Antoine. It was definitely him. What had Jean-Yves said his name was? Jack racked his brains. Altenberg. That was it. Albrecht Altenberg – the German physicist. It made sense. If you were dealing with radioactive material who else would you involve but your top nuclear physicist?

They were marched towards the hangar. It was a cavernous building and completely empty, but for one thing. Inside, there was a low concrete structure, a bit like an overgrown pillbox. It had two narrow, horizontally positioned windows built into its thick concrete walls at about eye level and between them there was a small, heavy-looking steel door. Next to the pillbox there was an area set aside for an array of engineering equipment.

A number of people were inside the hangar. There were soldiers, a few men dressed in white coats, who looked like doctors, and, strangely, two men dressed top to tail in all-in-one suits – a bit like the bio-hazard suits Jack had seen people in the army wearing. Jack was nervous enough already, but when he saw the men in these suits he started to feel scared. Very scared.

They were pushed towards the door in the concrete pillbox and a soldier heaved it open. Pendelshape tried to wriggle free, "Get off me...!"

A soldier jabbed his rifle butt into Pendelshape's ribs and bundled him through the door, doubled over in pain. Jack thought that he, Angus and Sophie were also about to be thrust inside the concrete box, but they were held back. From his position Jack could see that inside there was a small chamber which led directly to an inner door – smaller than the outer door. This door was opened and Jack saw Pendelshape thrown inside and down some concrete steps into another chamber that was partially below ground. Both doors were slammed shut with Pendelshape inside.

"You stay here!" a voice ordered. Jack, Angus and Sophie were pushed to the side and found themselves standing next to the narrow slit windows, peering down, directly into the concrete box. The glass was very thick and the concrete walls of the box must have been at least a metre wide. Inside, they could see Pendelshape staring up at them. He was sweating profusely and shouting up at them, a look of panic on his face – but from where they stood, they could hear absolutely nothing he was saying.

Jack glanced across to where Gottschalk, Altenberg and the other officers stood, also peering at Pendelshape inside the box. Gottschalk was having an animated conversation with Altenberg in German. In fact, it looked like they were arguing. The other officers and guards looked on, somewhat embarrassed, Jack thought, as Altenberg kept pointing into the box and then looking across at Jack and remonstrating with Gottschalk. Suddenly, Gottschalk shouted something at Altenberg and Altenberg went quiet, his face red with anger. Gottschalk barged passed the soldiers who were guarding Jack, Angus and Sophie and spoke directly to

Jack, his voice still quivering from the altercation with Altenberg.

"You have run out of time," he said, with menace in his voice. "We are going to run a little scientific test. I want you to watch carefully what happens inside the chamber. I would then like you to reconsider the information you are withholding."

Gottschalk turned away and gave a signal to the engineers who were sitting next to the scientific equipment and control panels. Inside the chamber, Jack saw a small recess open in the far wall. There was a flash and a puff of smoke and Jack felt an almost imperceptible vibration through his feet. The inside of the chamber filled with a fine dust. Slowly, the dust cleared. Jack could just make out the prostrate figure of Pendelshape through the settling dust on the bunker floor. His whole body was writhing from side to side and he pawed frantically at his mouth and throat. He was frothing a mixture of spittle and vomit and his face was turning purple. Slowly, the skin on his hands and face started to blister – as if he was burning. He was obviously screaming with pain, but Jack could still hear nothing through the thick concrete walls. In under a minute he had stopped moving and his lifeless eyes stared up at them, unblinking, from his position on the concrete floor. Pendelshape was dead. Sophie screamed and pounded the windows of the bunker. Unceremoniously, the guards dragged all three of them away to a corner of the hangar.

Angus was the first to come to his senses. "They've killed him…" he said in shock. "They've killed Pendelshape."

Jack was stunned, and then, it slowly dawned on him that the brutal execution of Pendelshape in the nuclear test bunker had been for their benefit.

"And one of us is next," he said.

Angus was shaking his head slowly from side to side, horrified by what he had seen.

Jack felt himself starting to panic, "But I don't have any information to give him…" He glanced over at the bunker and noticed that Gottschalk and Altenberg had started arguing again. This time, they were both shouting. The other officers were trying to calm them down. Suddenly, the argument seemed to reach some sort of conclusion and Gottschalk marched over to where Jack, Angus and Sophie were standing, closely followed by Altenberg.

Gottschalk addressed them, "Radioactive poisoning – it is not a nice way to die, as you have seen from our little test. Now, we have made an interesting discovery. It appears that two of the ringleaders are this young girl's parents. Quite extraordinary – a whole family of troublemakers." He glanced at Sophie, then at his watch. "They should have been here to witness our demonstration, but they seem to have been delayed. No matter, they will be here soon and this gives us some interesting possibilities for adding a little more… pressure. Eventually, one of you will talk."

Sophie's heart jumped – it was confirmation that her parents were alive. She tried to contain her joy. Gottschalk turned to Altenberg who was now standing next to him. "In the meantime I have one or two things to attend to, but my good friend, Professor Altenberg here, has asked for a quiet word with you. He has more patience than I and claims he can persuade you so there is no need for any more nonsense. Professor?"

"I will do my best *Brigadeführer*," Altenberg said through gritted teeth. "Give us a few minutes alone."

"Agreed," Gottschalk said, looking at his watch. "You have precisely five."

Gottschalk turned to the SS guards and said something in German. It sounded like an order. Gottschalk swivelled round and marched off with the guards, leaving Altenberg alone with them.

Altenberg spoke in a low, conspiratorial voice. "I thought we would have more time than this. But Gottschalk is worried that the British know about the German plans and things are now moving much faster than I expected. He is right to be worried," Altenberg looked over his shoulder, "I am working with British Intelligence. You have only one chance to escape. It is a slim chance. I'm afraid it's all I can do in the time. In a few minutes, there will be a little accident inside the hangar, but the distraction should be enough to give you a clear run to the gates. Take the jeep outside… on the backseat I have left a bag. It should contain all you need. There is a map which tells you one of my usual rendezvous points for the British agent. If no one is there, wait. Someone will come."

"But how…?"

"No time for questions, I'm afraid this is our only chance… Gottschalk means what he says."

Sophie pleaded, "But what about the others – my mother and father?"

Altenberg looked pained. "I believe they are being brought here under separate guard. They should have been here already. But if we wait it may be too late."

Sophie was desperate, "But…"

"I'm sorry… I will do my best for them, my dear. But please; save yourselves at least…"

Again, Altenberg glanced over his shoulder. Gottschalk was already on his way back to them.

"Well?" he demanded.

Altenberg pleaded with Gottschalk, "We are not barbarians, Gottschalk, this is not necessary... the girl... she is a child..."

But Gottschalk's mind was made up. "I see that despite your remonstrations, you have made as little progress with these fools as I have." He looked at his watch. "Fine. Let us make preparations."

But just as Gottschalk turned back to the concrete bunker, a loud explosion ripped through the back of the hanger. Then, all hell broke loose.

Angus was the first to react, "Come on!"

In the confusion, they sprinted through the hangar entrance and onto the concrete apron outside. The open-topped jeep was parked only a few metres away from the hangar – just where they had seen it when they had come in. Angus jumped into the driver's seat and Jack tumbled into the back.

"Have you driven one of these before?" Sophie shouted.

"No, but..."

"It's a Kübelwagen. I'll drive. It's not easy..."

"But..."

"Move over!" Sophie shouted.

Angus was taken aback, but obediently slid over to the passenger's side as Sophie plonked herself in the driver's seat. She fired the engine and slammed it into first gear. The jeep lurched towards the hangar and Sophie hauled hard on the steering wheel to avoid a collision. It spun round and there was a metallic crunch as Sophie thumped the gear lever into second.

"I thought you said you could drive one of these," Angus shouted.

"Did I?"

As Altenberg had promised, the surprise blast had given them the moment's distraction that they needed, but a couple of soldiers had already spotted them and were pointing and shouting at the jeep as it raced across the airfield. Then the firing started.

"They're shooting at us!" Jack shouted.

Just as the words left his mouth the windscreen of the Kübelwagen disintegrated and they were sprayed with shards of splintering glass. Sophie and Angus ducked down and for a moment Sophie drove blind as they powered on towards the wide gates of the airfield. Jack crouched low in the backseat, knowing that at any minute he was going to be peppered by the automatic rifle fire coming from the troops behind. Then, on the floor of the jeep, he spotted a canvas bag and a couple of metal objects. Impulsively, he reached down.

"Angus – I've got something here. Some sort of gun – there's a couple of them."

"Machine guns – is there any ammo?"

Jack opened the canvas bag.

"These? There's a few of them. "

"Give one here." Angus manipulated a long magazine into the gun. "You put the magazine in there, I think. It's got a folding stock – see?"

"No."

"Don't be an idiot." The jeep bumped across the airfield, topping forty miles an hour. Undeterred, Angus stood up on the front seat and rested the machine gun on the top edge of the windscreen's metal frame. He shouted back to Jack, "You fire from the back, I'll take the front. Go!"

Jack tried to copy Angus's instructions. He peered over the folded canvas roof which lay over the back of the Kübelwagen, and felt a bullet whip through the air millimetres from his face. He ducked down again, terrified, and scrunched himself into a ball in the back of the jeep.

Angus screamed back at him, "Come on Jack, get up! Fight back!"

At last something inside Jack snapped and he was suddenly bursting with energy. He climbed up from his foetal position and stood with one leg resting on the back of the jeep and the other on the back seat. The whole airfield unfolded before him, the hangar fading into the distance. A second Kübelwagen was now on their tail, followed by a lumbering armoured car and an army truck. The soldiers behind them kept up their fire but they were now over four hundred metres away and their shots were increasingly speculative. Jack didn't care – he squeezed the trigger and let rip with the machine gun. In less than five seconds, the thirty-two round magazine was empty.

"Reload!" Angus shouted.

Jack pawed in the bag to locate a second magazine. They had nearly reached the main gate of the aerodrome. It was flanked by a guard post and a machine-gun emplacement protected by sandbags. Soldiers were running to man the emplacement and to pull the gate shut. Angus fired randomly from the front of the jeep as they powered towards the gate. As if in a trance, Jack squeezed the trigger again, and he felt the weapon shudder in his hands. His mouth opened and he knew that he was shouting, but he could not hear himself. It was as if he was in a dream, in slow motion, keeping his finger on the trigger, he moved the machine gun, slung at waist level, in an arc from side to side. He was vaguely conscious of people, soldiers, running and diving for cover, as the jeep raced onwards.

"Get down and hold on!" Sophie shouted.

Jack snapped out of his trance. The gate was still half open and it was only two metres away. He dropped back into the seat and clung on. It didn't look like the gap was big enough, but Sophie kept her foot flat on the accelerator. There was a screech of metal as the jeep burst through the closing gate and onto the woodland track beyond.

"You can drive any time you want," Angus bawled out joyfully, putting a friendly arm around Sophie.

Jack snatched a look behind. "They're still tailing us!"

Angus swivelled round in time to see the second Kübelwagen pass through the gates, right on their tail. Behind that, the army truck lumbered and swayed through the checkpoint, belching black diesel smoke and straining to keep up.

"Not good. Do we have any more clips?"

"What's a clip?" Jack asked.

Angus groaned, "Magazine clips – the long black things with all the bullets in them."

"There are two more." Jack pulled them out, handed one to Angus and hooked the canvas bag over his shoulder.

"Right, I'm coming over to join you." With that Angus clambered over his seat and stood next to Jack in the back.

"What do I do – just keep going?" Sophie asked.

Jack looked ahead. The road was quite good – a rough gritted track. But it was not clear how far the woodland extended or where the road led. Up ahead, Jack spied a fork in the road. A second, much rougher track led directly into the woodland.

"Take the right-hand track. The big truck won't be able to follow us and we'll have a better chance of escaping into the woodland. If we join up onto a main road or something, we'll be sitting ducks…"

"They're closing…!" Angus shouted. He had already replaced his magazine with a fresh one and was crouching down low on the back seat of the Kübelwagen, resting his gun on the back edge and pointing it at the other jeep which was now only fifty metres behind.

"There are four of them… what do we do?"

Angus replied in his best Rambo, "Spray 'em," and the muzzle of his gun flamed.

"You missed."

Suddenly Sophie turned sharply into the right-hand road and the track became bumpier – dust spewed up behind the rear tyres and Sophie grappled with the steering wheel to keep them on the track. She gunned the engine, maintaining full revs and, inside, they bounced around like toddlers on a trampoline. The jeep behind was having similar problems with the rough terrain – they could see it lurching from side to side as the driver wrestled it along the badly pitted track.

Suddenly, they reached the edge of the woodland and emerged onto a broad, low ridge that looked out over a flattish valley.

In the far distance, Jack saw the spire of a church in the middle of a village. The track wound its way down the ridge and then over a small hump-backed bridge set at an angle over some sort of depression at the bottom of the valley. At first, it was not clear why the bridge was there. Sophie slowed down, taking stock of the landscape stretching before them. The engine of the jeep idled.

"What are you doing, Sophie?" Angus shouted. "Keep going or they'll catch up." They could hear the other jeep approaching from the woodland behind. In a few seconds it would be there. But Sophie wasn't listening. Instead, she was staring off into the middle distance, her face set in deep concentration. She moved her head slowly to the right to look at the bridge below them. It was about three hundred metres away and the track followed a single broad bend up to the bridge and then over and on to the village in the distance. She turned her head back to the left and Jack followed her gaze until he realised what she was looking at.

In the distance, a plume of steam and smoke was pumping into the sky, forming a thick cloud that spread in a continuous streak across the landscape. Partially hidden from view in a shallow cutting, a goods train was rattling its way across the valley.

"Come on, Sophie, what are you waiting for?" Angus pressed. He looked round, anxiously gauging the progress of their pursuers.

The enemy jeep emerged from the woodland. Sophie turned round to Angus and Jack in the backseat. She had a strangely calm expression on her face, but her eyes twinkled mischievously.

"Boys – it is time to use the last of those bullets… and then I want you to hold on. I want you to hold on very tightly indeed."

Jack had no idea what she meant. But no sooner had she spoken, than she was revving the engine of the Kübelwagen one last time and dropping the clutch so the vehicle shot forward. Angus didn't need to be told twice and once again he let rip with the machine gun from the rear of the jeep. Jack crouched down copying him and the approaching German jeep slewed sideways to avoid the maelstrom. Sophie accelerated as they belted down the escarpment. The track curved before the bridge and rose at a slight angle over the railway. Sophie rounded the bend and careered up to the bridge just as the lumbering black mass of the goods train thundered beneath. It was at this point, with the wagons flashing past that Jack realised, with horror, what Sophie was about to do. She hauled down on the steering wheel and the jeep veered dangerously onto a new trajectory, which launched it from the edge of the road, through a low side wall and into the air. The jeep's engine, free of the friction of its wheels on the road, screamed as if making a wild bid for freedom. Jack felt himself becoming airborne as they flew off the track. Two seconds later the jeep landed with an eviscerating crunch on top of the penultimate wagon of the train as it emerged from under the bridge. The jeep bounced once, then again, and then slid along the top of the train until it ground to a halt.

For a moment Jack sat in the back seat, on top of the train, in stunned silence. They were in a German army jeep perched high up on a goods train rattling through the French countryside at forty miles an hour. And somehow they were alive. But ahead, Jack spotted a new danger. They train was heading for a tunnel. He was the first to react.

"Get out!" he cried.

The three of them clambered over the back of the Kübelwagen and onto the roof of the train. Jack looked back – they were bearing down on the tunnel at a dizzying pace. They ran to the end of the wagon and from there Jack peered down at the railway sleepers below as they flashed by at a frightening speed.

There was a narrow ladder at the back of the wagon. "We can use that to climb down!" Sophie went first, quickly followed by Angus. Jack turned, put his foot on the ladder and paused. From this position he had a clear view of the approaching tunnel and the jeep perched up high on top of the train. First the engine entered and the smoke and steam blew back out of the tunnel. The wagons followed and suddenly the jeep slammed into the arced brickwork above the tunnel entrance and vaporised. Jack felt Angus haul him down, just as various components of the disintegrating Kübelwagen flew towards him like shrapnel from an exploding shell. Suddenly, it was pitch dark and they were gasping for breath in the smoke and steam of the tunnel. When they emerged, seconds later, there was no trace of the jeep at all.

They clung on to the ladder for dear life as the train rattled on through the countryside.

"What do we do now?" Jack shouted.

"We jump," Angus replied.

Refuge

Jack rolled over five times before coming to halt, wedged in a large gorse bush. He was scratched and shaken, but otherwise OK. He looked back down the track as the train shrank into the distance. Then, hearing a groan behind him, he turned round. Angus was upside down in a second gorse bush, struggling to free himself. "Get me out of this stupid thing."

Jack manoeuvred himself over to Angus and tried to support his friend as he disentangled himself from the bush. Without warning, the bush released him and Jack tumbled back with Angus on top of him.

Sophie appeared, looking down at them. "Enjoying yourselves, boys?"

They scrambled to their feet.

"We can't stay here – they will send a search party down the railway line soon."

"OK then, how about we scramble up there?"

Jack nodded up at the steep bank of the railway cutting and they started to climb. From the top, they could just see the train wending its way onwards, puffing white clouds into the clear blue summer sky. In front of them lay rolling farmland.

"There!"

Sophie pointed to a dilapidated barn next to a copse at the other side of a broad field. Keeping their eyes peeled, they picked their way across the field towards the timber-framed building. Angus heaved open the heavy door and looked inside.

"No one. We can hide here for a while."

One end of the barn was stacked with old hay and the other with rusty farm equipment. Angus pulled out two of the hay bales and they plonked themselves down.

"Anything else in that?" Angus asked. He pointed at the bag from the Kübelwagen that had miraculously remained strapped to Jack's shoulders.

"Our friend Altenberg has thought of everything."

Jack pulled out an apple, then some bread and sausage and finally a bar of chocolate. German chocolate.

"Someone's lunch. And there's water."

They divided the contents of the bag between the three of them. The prospect of food had a remarkably energising effect and soon Jack felt his spirits lift.

"Have to tell you, Sophie," Angus spoke as he chomped through the sausage, "what you just did was amazing... that jump..."

But Sophie had wrapped her arms around herself and was staring at the straw and dust on the bottom of the barn, brooding. It was as if she had not even heard Angus.

Jack reached out tentatively and touched her hand, "You all right?"

She flinched. Her brown eyes were moist and her face was set in a grim expression. After a while, she said quietly through clenched teeth, "I keep seeing it in my head... your friend in the bunker, Pendelshape. I keep thinking they're going to do the same thing to Mum and Dad."

It had taken all their energy just to stay alive in the last twenty-four hours and Jack had blanked out the dreadful scene of the men being machine-gunned at the chateau... only to be followed by the gruesome spectacle of Pendelshape's death from radioactive poisoning. Now it all came back to him, as it had to Sophie. He wanted to reach out to her, to somehow share her pain, words came and went through his head, but they all seemed trivial and inadequate.

"We need to try and rescue Mum and Dad..." she said. "Before they kill them."

Jack wanted to give Sophie hope. She had saved their lives and he wanted to do something for her in return. He put his arm round Sophie's shoulders. "Sophie, Altenberg said he'd do what he could. He helped us. Maybe he can help them. But for now we need to get to the rendezvous point where Altenberg meets with British Intelligence. It's our best chance, and the best chance to save your parents too. It's only a matter of time before the SS rip the countryside apart looking for us." Jack peered into the bag again. "Altenberg said that he left a map in here..." He rummaged about. "Got it!"

Jack unfurled the map on the floor of the barn. "This way up, I think." He studied it carefully. "It's definitely of round here. Look – there's the airfield... and the railway."

"Villiers-sur-Oise is right over there in the corner," Angus added.

"Look. I think Altenberg has marked it. A little village with a church – St Augustine – and he's marked a circle nearby in the woods, next to the river. That must be the rendezvous."

"So we must be around here do you think?" Angus pointed and ran his finger along a line on the map. "So that road… I guess if we just try and keep walking in that direction, we'll hit it."

"It's what… maybe five miles east? It's walkable."

"Won't everywhere be crawling with SS? The three of us together – we would be recognised."

"Well, we certainly can't hang around here, we're too near the railway." Jack stood up. "We need to get going."

They sneaked out of the barn and walked down the farm track, staying close to the hedge on one side and keeping a watch all around them. The sun glinted down from a clear sky and for the first time in a while, Jack felt a little spring in his step. If they could make it to St Augustine and the rendezvous with the British agents who were working with Altenberg, surely, finally, they would be safe.

After a few hundred yards they crested a low ridge and the road marked on the map loomed into view. It was quite busy. There were people, vehicles and animals moving along the road. There were crude farm carts hauled by horses, carrying entire families with their possessions. There were people walking with suitcases and bags. Mixed in with the refugees, the remains of what seemed like an entire French infantry regiment extended for kilometres along the road – weaponless, bedraggled and defeated. Jack, Angus and Sophie joined them on the road, and nobody really seemed to notice them.

"I think it is that way…" Jack whispered to Angus and Sophie.

"Should we split up or something? We're more obvious walking together."

"Good idea, Sophie. Let's try and stay a few hundred metres apart… without losing sight of one another."

Proceeding in this way, they did their best to blend in with the plodding stream of refugees. Once, a German army truck nosed its way through the crowd, blaring its horn. Jack put his head down and it rumbled past. It seemed they were well hidden among the other travellers. They kept walking for what seemed like hours. Finally, the traffic on the road started to thin out. The sun was getting hotter and Jack began to feel very thirsty. Then, up ahead he spotted a pitted track that turned off the main road into some woodland. There was a tatty sign by the roadside, with the name 'St Augustine' painted in peeling letters. Jack's heart gave a little jump. He turned round to check on the progress of Angus and Sophie who, as agreed, continued to keep a safe distance. They were still in sight. Jack waited a moment and turned off the road and up the lane. A tiny chapel appeared on the left and, but for a few other cottages, that seemed to be all there was to the hamlet of St Augustine. Jack remembered from the map that he needed to take another track – it proved to be almost completely overgrown – past the chapel and down towards the woods near the river. The trees finally gave some shelter from the burning sun and Jack waited for Angus and Sophie to catch him up. In ten minutes they were together. They were tired and hot.

"It's quiet here," Angus said.

"Yes – no one's around. I'll check the map, but I think we just keep following this track until it reaches the river."

They continued walking until the woods became thicker. Suddenly, the track petered out and they found themselves in a small glade. Ahead was a river, the Oise, maybe. The water drifted past languidly, sparkling in the sun. It seemed like they had found the only peaceful place left in northern France. It was odd to think that a little further north, only a few weeks before, the French army had been ripped apart by Guderian and Rommel's rampant panzer divisions.

"What a great place," Jack said.

"You know what? I don't care – I'm doing it," Angus said. Jack and Sophie watched in surprise as Angus stripped down to his underwear and then sprinted across the glade towards the river. He launched himself into the water.

Jack grinned at Sophie, "What the hell. You coming?"

They dropped their clothes by the riverbank, and soon all three of them were splashing around in the cool water. It felt incredibly good after the long walk in the sun, and for a moment they didn't have a care.

After a while, Jack pulled himself up from the bank and sat watching, dripping wet and panting for breath, as Angus and Sophie attempted underwater handstands out in the middle of the river. Jack laughed at them as he towelled himself down with his shirt and slipped his trousers back on, and at first he did not hear the noise of the old grocery van approaching behind him through the woods. The van turned into the glade and stopped. Suddenly Jack heard the engine and, startled, he jumped to his feet and swivelled round. The van bumped its way across the glade and drew to a halt. Jack's heart was pumping. For a moment he considered running… one word in his poor French would arouse unwelcome interest, but before he could do anything, a man climbed out of the cab. He wore a floppy blue beret over his wavy blonde hair. His loose-fitting work clothes covered a white shirt that was stained with sweat and grime. He didn't look much like a grocer. The man was slim and had piercing blue eyes and fine features. But he looked tired and obviously had not shaved for several days. He approached tentatively, and as he got closer Jack realised that there was something familiar about him, but could not think where he may have seen the man before. As he approached, the anxious expression on his face changed, firstly to one of confusion and then, finally, into a broad, exuberant grin. He was now running towards Jack, his arms outstretched. He spoke in perfect English.

"Jack! It can't be…"

Jack stared back, speechless, then he started to run towards the man, shaking with emotion.

"Dad?"

A Grocer's Tale

Jack stared at his father, dumbstruck. He had so many questions flying through his head, he thought it would explode. Christie enveloped Jack in a bear hug. "Thank God... it's incredible... miraculous..." he stepped back, "but how?"

Jack was excited and incredibly relieved to see his dad, but also confused... very confused.

"It's a long story, Dad, but I tell you, we nearly didn't make it..."

Christie shook his head. "I'm sorry Jack, it's all my fault..."

Jack shrugged. "I guess we're here, and alive. That's the main thing, isn't it?"

Christie grinned and hugged Jack again. "Yes, Jack, you're right. But how did you get here? You must have accessed the VIGIL Taurus... but when I came to 1940 I thought that VIGIL was finished, I was so worried, but I never imagined for one minute..."

"I'll tell you all about it – and then you can tell me how you come to be working for British Intelligence; although I think I have an idea..."

"That's a cover story," he glanced towards the river, "but these two friends of yours, are they from VIGIL too... did anyone else escape? I tell you, we could use the help." Angus and Sophie were now way out in the middle of the river but had spotted Jack and his father on the bank and were quickly making their way back.

"That's Angus, you know, my friend from home. There's no one else from VIGIL here. We don't know what happened to them – we only just got away. The girl with Angus is Sophie. She's not VIGIL, she's from here, from 1940. She has no idea about who we really are and she won't know who you are."

Christie thought for a moment. "OK. Best keep it that way. It could lead to serious complications if she knew the truth. We'll need to try and distract Angus and have a word with him when they get up here... and you'll both need to keep quiet about who I really am."

"You're working with him, aren't you? Altenberg, I mean. He was the one who saved us. He told us to meet here. Does *he* know who you really are?"

"No. He thinks I'm British Intelligence. I followed Pendelshape back to 1940 and I discovered the Nazis had got hold of his plans. I had to work out a way to stop them. I discovered Albrecht Altenberg was leading the scientific effort. An obvious choice for the Nazis, but I knew who he was from History books and I couldn't believe he could be sympathetic to them. I took a gamble and made contact, posing as British Intelligence. He was scared at first, but he's come round. It's useful that I know something about science. We get on well. He finds himself forced to help the Nazis and is horrified at the prospect of arming rockets with nuclear weapons. If the Nazis find out what he really thinks they will kill him for sure."

"Dad – Pendelshape – they kidnapped him in London and brought him here. Did you know that? We were trying to follow him. Gottschalk had him killed – in some radioactive bunker.

It happened this morning. Gottschalk called it a test. They made us watch; it was horrific…"

Christie stared at Jack, "Oh my God… Pendelshape… dead? Altenberg said they'd captured an English scientist and brought him to Villiers – it was just a few days ago. He arrived with Petersen. He was sure it was the man Petersen had sourced the blueprints from. It had to be Pendelshape. I'm surprised Gottschalk risked leaving him in Britain for so long. There was nothing I could do…" His head dropped. "He and I, well, we had our differences, and by the end I despised him for the risks he took. But now, dead…" he stared down at the ground shaking his head. "It's a terrible waste."

"Dad – Sophie and Angus are coming over now. It's all true then, what Pendelshape told us, about the rocket and the nuclear weapon… here at Villiers?"

"Yes. The Nazis have made very quick progress with all Pendelshape's blueprints. When France was defeated, they started the next phase of their plan and moved all their equipment to the forward base here in Villiers. It is a good spot. Quiet, but with good rail and road access. It's near Paris but has the protection of the forward Luftwaffe fields between here and the Channel. Altenberg and I started to work out a plan to stop the Nazis, but then those hotheads from the Network launched an attack. I should have known better. I knew there was Resistance activity in the area, in fact I thought I might need their help. But now those poor people have gone and got themselves killed and it's going to make things much more difficult."

"We met up with the Resistance when we got to Paris… "

Jack told him. "Sophie and her parents helped us. It's a long story… anyway her parents got caught up in the raid yesterday and so did we. It was awful, the SS killed a bunch of them; we saw it all from the woods. We think that Gottschalk is still holding Sophie's parents prisoner. Sophie's beside herself with worry…"

Sophie and Angus had hauled themselves out of from the river, sopping wet, and were approaching cautiously.

"Dad – they're coming…" said Jack. "Let's hope Angus doesn't clock who you really are straight away and blow it in front of Sophie."

"Yes, you're right, you'll need to get him on his own, explain things…" replied Christie.

Jack stepped forward. "Guys, this is the contact Altenberg wanted us to meet. He's called Tom – he's from British Intelligence."

Angus looked at Christie curiously, but before he could say anything, Christie put out his hand. "Very good to meet you both. It's Angus and Sophie isn't it? Looks like you need to get dry. Jack – why don't you and Angus get some food from the back of my van – looks like you need it." Christie gave Jack a surreptitious wink. "I'm going to try and get a fire going. Sophie, perhaps you can help me? Then you can dry off, and we'll have a chance to talk about everything properly."

A while later they were still sitting round the fire, chewing on the remains of the food and drinking coffee as Christie talked. He looked at his watch suddenly.

"Altenberg and I usually arrange to meet at this time every

couple of days. This is one of the rendezvous points. But he's overdue. With everything that has happened today it's not surprising. I just hope it's nothing more sinister. We can't do anything without his help. He's my only contact on the inside."

They stared at the embers of the fire as the evening sun started to set. Suddenly they heard the puttering of a motor scooter engine. Christie's face lit up.

"That's got to be him."

The scooter bumped into the glade and a man jumped off, pulling off his goggles and skullcap as he ran towards them. It was Altenberg. He was flustered, but he looked very relieved to see them.

"Tom… I got here as soon as I could. It was not easy…" He looked at Jack, Angus and Sophie. "You escaped… incredible… I am so relieved."

Christie put out his hands to welcome him. "You've no idea how happy you've made me, Albrecht. Will you have some coffee… or something stronger, maybe?"

"Something stronger, I think Tom, we will need nerves of steel for what we have to do now." He sat down next to the fire as Christie broke another branch and pushed it into the flames. "I have news," Altenberg continued. "Gottschalk is worried. He is very suspicious that British Intelligence is onto him. He is cursing that he left Pendelshape alone in London so long with only Petersen to keep an eye on him. First there was the raid by the French resistance, and now your incredible escape. He thinks maybe the charge that exploded in the hangar was not an accident. He fears there is an insider and he's worried that maybe next there will be an RAF raid, or another attack. He has increased security and the Luftwaffe are mounting regular patrols… but that's not all…"

"What is it, Albrecht?"

"Gottschalk has decided to bring forward the launch. He got the authorisation from Hitler and the top brass when they were all in Paris a couple of days ago. There is now a big race to get everything ready…"

"When? When is the launch?"

"It's tomorrow."

Christie's head dropped. "But we're not ready. We have no other help. It's just us."

"We have no choice, Tom, we have to make a plan. Jack – do you still have that map I left for you?"

Jack pulled the map out of the bag and spread it out on the grass.

"OK. Here is Villiers-sur-Oise and this is where they're going to launch the rocket," Altenberg began. "There are some limestone caves there which hold the various stores and then nearby are the concrete assembly houses we have built opposite the cave entrance for preparing the rocket prior to launch. The launch pad itself is in a special clearing in the woods – there. The rocket is contained in a silo, under the concrete base. It gives better protection from the air. The whole site is linked by a narrow-gauge railway."

Jack interrupted. "It's launching tomorrow – what's the target?"

"We think it's Portsmouth," Christie said, "on the south coast of England. It's a big city and a key naval base. France has just surrendered and the British army have been evacuated from

Dunkirk. Britain stands alone. If Hitler can also get Britain to surrender, then he has won."

"Thousands of people will die…" Altenberg added. "Britain will have no choice but to surrender. We have to stop it. And I think there is a way, but we have to be completely sure. I think I know how to swap the radioactive payload. I am in charge of all the procedures for that. But I am worried that something might happen to me before I do the swap – or that it might go wrong. I think we need to work out a way to get you into the base so we can destroy the rocket and the assembly areas as well. That way we make it fail-safe; we can be sure. With the accelerated plan, they will be doing the final assembly all through tonight, but the rocket won't be transported from the assembly to the silo for final fuelling and launching until later tomorrow morning. Tom, you have explosives I think? If you can set them to destroy the assembly blocks we will be absolutely certain of success." He opened his rucksack. "Here, I managed to bring a uniform, there are many people on site, and new people too, now the security is being tightened… I don't think you will be noticed."

"I have enough explosives to take out half of France, Albrecht, but there is only one problem…"

"What?"

"Access. Even with a uniform I don't think I can get in to the site with explosives undetected. They'll be searching everyone. Especially after all that's happened. It would be a suicide mission."

It was a dead end.

Then suddenly Sophie spoke up. "We know how to get into the launch site," there was quiet confidence in her voice.

"Last night after the raid, the Nazis must have thought we got through the perimeter fence. But we didn't."

Christie's eyebrows arched. "You've been to the launch site? How did you get in?"

"Through the graveyard, of course…" she replied.

Return

It was too dangerous to approach the graveyard directly from Villiers. Instead, they had carried several bags from Tom Christie's van cross-country for what seemed like miles. Following his secret rendezvous with them at St Augustine's, Altenberg had returned to the V-2 base as quickly as he could. They were now deep in the woods, near the perimeter wall of the graveyard. It was getting dark and all was quiet. Jack was very tired. The idea of re-entering the cave sent a shiver down his spine. They gathered round as Christie went through the plan with them one last time.

"Your job is to help me carry this stuff through the catacomb and down through the cave. Once there, I will change into the German uniform and make my way through from the back of the cave to the front storage area. It'll be very early in the morning, but there will be work going on, so I have to be careful." He opened his backpack. "This is one of the explosive charges and a detonator. I'll try and plant one of these in each of the assembly sheds timed to go off after we have escaped. I've got enough to take out half of this hill."

"Cool," Angus said enthusiastically. His respect for Jack's dad was rising by the moment.

Christie grinned. "You set the timer and just stick the charge onto the target… if you take that piece off you'll see it's sticky – it will attach to just about anything. A little modification I made myself."

"Altenberg says the launch is scheduled for early afternoon. There is a very carefully planned sequence of events prior to launch. They'll make the final checks and assemblies in the morning, which will include inserting the dirty bomb in the special payload compartment inside the rocket. Altenberg is going to try and disrupt this process."

Jack listened intently.

"We will wait out the early part of tonight in the cave so I can go in before dawn and plant the explosives. I want you to wait for me. Then, we'll return here via the tunnel and make our way back up to the chateau. When the explosion goes off all hell will break loose, so Sophie, that's when I'm hoping we can get to the chateau and try to free your parents. My promise to you is that we will *try*. OK?"

Sophie nodded.

"Assuming all goes according to plan we'll then make our way back to Paris," he looked around. "Is that all clear?"

"Right – let's go. Keep very quiet."

In a moment they were inside the graveyard. The colour had already leached from the evening sky and the gravestones were washed in a shadowy monochrome.

Jack whispered, "The mausoleum is over there – in the corner – through those yews."

As they sneaked across the graveyard towards the mausoleum, Jack had a sense of déjà vu – everything was just as it had been the day before. They opened the metal gate and descended into the crypt. Angus and Christie switched on their torches.

"This place is even worse when you can actually see it."

"Keep your voice down – where's the entrance that leads to the caves?"

"Over here." Sophie had picked her way over to the far side and was crouching down. There was a dark hole where Angus had broken down the old wooden door the night before. They ducked their heads through the small doorway and crept into the passage beyond. Jack tried not to look at the grim sight of the human bones and skulls in each of the recesses along the walls. After a while the gradient started to descend and the passageway became more dilapidated. Soon they reached the shelf high up in the underground cavern. The great swirling stalactites and stalagmites were even more impressive by the light of the electric torches.

"The ladder is over here," Jack said.

At the bottom of the cave, they walked on for a bit and finally Christie called them to a halt.

"This will do. We'll hunker down here for the night. It's not going to be particularly pleasant – but it is only for a few hours."

They wrapped themselves up in the blankets that they had brought with them as best they could and used the bags as pillows. Christie handed round the last of his chocolate and the water.

"Sorry – it's all I've got left."

The cave was cold and uncomfortable, but they were all tired and soon Jack could hear Angus and Sophie breathing heavily in a deep sleep, exhausted by their tumultuous day. The torches were off and it was pitch dark in the cave. But despite his fatigue and aching limbs, Jack could not get to sleep. Random worries and thoughts churned backwards and forwards through his head. Each minute that ticked away, he knew they came closer to the point where his dad would leave them to complete the mission. He had played down the dangers, but Jack knew that he was risking his life, in fact, they all were.

"Dad – you still awake?" Jack whispered.

"Still here, Jack. I forgot one thing."

"What?"

"The time phones. I have got mine with me. I want you to take Pendelshape's." Jack felt his dad pass something over to him in the darkness. It had the familiar smooth surface of the precious time-travel device. "These time phones connect to the Revisionist Taurus. When I left there were only two of the team left. The rest were on the VIGIL raid. One of them is a friend of mine – he's stayed loyal – he tipped me off about Pendelshape and helped me get back into the Revisionist base. The Revisionist Taurus will automatically poll its linked time phones whenever there is a signal. It's standard procedure and means we can initiate a transfer when the yellow light is on. With Pendelshape's time phone, if anything happens to me, well, you and Angus have a way back."

"Dad, I'm scared. What's going to happen to you – to all of us – tomorrow."

For a moment Jack's father didn't answer. There was just the black silence of the cave.

"It's going to be OK, Jack. We've both been in tougher spots than this. You just need to concentrate on what you've got to do.

We'll be fine. Soon we'll be home and it will be over – for good this time. I promise you that."

"I hope so Dad, 'cos I'm not sure I can take much more of this."

Jack could hear his father's voice closer now, whispering in the darkness. "I'm sorry. That I've got you, all of you, into all this… trouble. It's not what I wanted. I thought I could control them, but then Pendelshape… he kind of went off the rails… and ever since then, well, the Revisionists have become fanatical. They expelled me. I can't have anything to do with them. We'll get through tomorrow, and then we'll get home, and we can finish it for good this time."

"You'll give up, you mean? Give up trying to change history – making everything better?"

"It's been a difficult journey for me, Jack. I guess I have discovered that the future is more important than the past: our future. I realise that now. We will have to make some important decisions – we can't let this happen again."

Jack felt the comfort of his father's words. For the first time in a long time, it felt like someone else was sharing the load. Jack remembered the strange image of himself next to his father, which he had seen from the Taurus Transfer Chamber. The image was stronger than ever in his head. Maybe that time was drawing closer. He wanted to tell his father about it, but something held him back. For some reason he was scared that telling him about it would jeopardise everything. Maybe it was irrational, but that was how he felt.

After a while, he pulled the blanket tight around his shoulders and slid into a deep sleep.

In what only seemed like minutes, Jack woke up with a gentle hand on his shoulder. "It's time."

His bones ached from the cold.

"Give me some light, while I get changed." Christie stripped down and pulled on the German uniform. He looked at his watch. "Fine. Now we need to wake the others."

Jack leaned over and shook Angus and Sophie, who were still wrapped up, mummy-like, in the blankets.

"What's going on?" Angus murmured, semi-conscious.

In a minute they were all wide awake and packing up, ready to get started.

"Are we ready?" Christie said.

Slowly, they crept forward. The cave tapered into a passageway and then led through the mini-caves.

Jack whispered, "I think we're near. Yes. Shine the torch there. The front caves are blocked off by this planking – but that one over there is loose. You can get through."

Christie flashed his torch at the planks. He turned to them with final instructions and looked at his watch.

"Five-thirty a.m. Angus – make sure your watch is synchronised with mine – right?"

"Done," Angus said.

"OK – listen carefully," Christie said. "I'm going through and then I'll make my way to the storage caves at the front. The assembly sheds are across the clearing only about fifty metres from the cave entrance, right?"

"Yes," Jack and Angus spoke together.

Christie continued, "As Altenberg said, everyone will be busy preparing the rocket launch – they're not going to worry about another guard. I aim to plant a charge behind each of the assembly sheds on a timer. Then I'm going to return here and we'll retrace our steps through the caves and up into the graveyard. We should be well away before the whole place goes up. I'm leaving you a gun and one of the charges – just in case."

Jack studied his father's face in the fading light of the torch. He looked as tired as Jack felt. "You sure about this, Dad… Tom, I mean…?" Jack corrected himself quickly, hoping he hadn't revealed his dad's identity to Sophie.

"Yes Jack. I'm sure. It'll all be fine – OK?"

They nodded.

"Now, here's the thing," he continued. "I am allowing myself a maximum of one hour plus thirty minutes contingency. If I'm not back before seven a.m. you must go."

And with that, Christie crouched down, squeezed his way past the loose planking and was gone.

Day of Vengeance

"**H**e's late," Angus said. "It's seven-ten."

"We must go," Sophie said. "My parents…"

Jack was fraught. "We can't just leave him."

"Jack, it is what he said," Sophie tapped her foot impatiently. "We must go. I am sure he will be very close behind. You must help me now."

Jack pushed her away.

"I'm sorry, Sophie. I lost him once and I'm not going to lose him again. I'm going after him."

Sophie looked at Jack with a puzzled expression. She had no idea what Jack was talking about. But she didn't have time to question him, because he had already ducked through the hole in the wall. Angus whispered angrily after him, "Jack!"

But it was too late. Jack was gone. Angus rolled his eyes. "Come on Sophie – otherwise he's just going to get himself into trouble."

Angus set off and Sophie followed, muttering something to herself in French.

They hurried through from the back of the cave and soon found themselves at the front again with its stacked crates. They crept along the side behind the crates, just as before. The gates at the front of the cave had been left open and the light from a clear summer's day poured in, straining their eyes. It seemed to be eerily quiet. Gingerly, they approached the entrance.

Jack crouched down and peaked out from the front of the storeroom. The scene before him was very different in daylight, but his recollection of the broad features of the site just before they had been caught was accurate. The entrance to the storerooms, which led into the limestone cave system, was built into a steep-sided, wooded hill. The chateau must be somewhere on the hill above them. There was thick woodland all around but immediately in front was a clearing. The four concrete assembly houses were opposite and to the left, across the clearing. Each was about seven meters high and about the same width. There was a narrow-gauge railway built into the ground, which ran from the assembly houses and then curved away along a track that disappeared into the woodland beyond. Outside the assembly houses was a crane. The doors of the assembly houses were open. There was no one about.

Angus crept up beside Jack. "It's completely dead – I thought there were supposed to be people, soldiers, engineers. Where is everyone?"

Suddenly, they heard the sound of an engine coming towards them. They pulled back from the entrance and ducked down behind a crate near the door. The noise grew louder and Jack poked his head above the top of the crate. Approaching fast, from the track into the woods, an army motorbike and sidecar appeared, followed by a Kübelwagen. They drove into the clearing and Jack's heart sank when he saw who was in the back of the jeep. He whispered to the others, "They've got Dad!"

"Christie – he's your father? But…?"

Jack suddenly realised his mistake, "I'll explain later…"

Angus fingered his backpack. "Jack – we've got the other gun in here… and the other explosive charge…"

"We don't stand a chance – there are two of them on the bike and two in the jeep. We've had it."

The Kübelwagen pulled up right outside the entrance to the storeroom, partially blocking the entrance. The motorbike and sidecar pulled up alongside, puttering away in neutral. Jack was frozen to the spot. He knew they should run to the back of the storeroom and escape through the cave… but then he saw his dad's face. It was bruised and puffed up and blood was dripping from a cut in his cheek. He had been beaten up. The soldiers dragged him from the back of the Kübelwagen and onto the floor of the storeroom. His hands were tied behind him and, unable to break his fall, his head hit the ground with a crack. The four SS soldiers stood above him. One was an officer and he leaned down and screamed something in German millimetres from Christie's ear. Jack heard his father moan. The officer clicked his fingers and one of the soldiers slammed his boot into Christie's stomach. Christie screamed.

Jack suddenly lost it. He grabbed the pack and snatched out the pistol. Leaping onto the crate, he fired wildly into the group of soldiers. The first round struck the nearest soldier in the leg and he reeled backwards. The next three bullets went wide, but the fifth caught the officer in the shoulder and he sank to his knees, clutching himself in pain. The other two soldiers twisted round, reaching for their weapons. Jack pulled the trigger again and then twice more. But the gun was empty. He was standing high up on the crate, gun dangling uselessly from his hand, as the two soldiers brought their machine guns to bear on him. But Angus and Sophie moved quickly. Sophie climbed, catlike, onto a second crate and, as Jack prepared to die, she hurtled through the air with one leg fully extended and her other tucked beneath her. Her father may have criticised elements of Sophie's technique, but as her outstretched foot connected with the jaw of the unfortunate SS soldier, there was no doubt, that had Jean-Yves been there, he would be have been proud. The gun flew from the soldier's hands and he tumbled backwards with Sophie on top of him, before cracking his head on the floor of the storeroom. He did not move.

Meanwhile, Angus had decided to take a less graceful approach to the problem of the final SS soldier. He shot through the gap between the crates like a frenzied bull and propelled himself into the air. His body was horizontal as he slammed into the soldier, who careened across the floor before coming to rest somewhere on the other side of the storeroom with Angus on top of him.

Jack jumped down from the crate and held his father's head in his hands.

"Dad – are you OK?"

His father moaned. Jack looked around at the mayhem. Angus had already picked up one of the soldier's guns and was holding it at the ready.

"There's some rope next to that crate – we can tie them up."

"Jack…"

Jack turned back to his father who was trying to say something. "What Dad? What do you need?"

"I'm OK… a broken rib… it's nothing… the rocket…"

"What?"

"The rocket… we have to stop the rocket. It's going to launch."

Christie tried to haul himself up, but he was too shaken.

"Lie there for a minute, Dad, what are you talking about?"

"They are about to launch the rocket…" he spoke in a whisper, obviously in pain. "They've accelerated the launch sequence… it's even earlier than Altenberg expected… I planted the charges, but they won't go off in time. We only have a few minutes."

Jack was flabbergasted. "What? But how? We have to get out of here."

Christie grabbed Jack's hand, understanding his desperation, "But I don't know what's happened to Altenberg… the payload… he won't have had time to change it. If it launches, thousands will die. It's not meant to be…"

"How? How do we stop it?"

"Take the last charge. Take the sidecar – the rocket silo is at the end of the track, through the woods. Drop the charge into the silo. You will have a clear run. Everyone is inside the observation areas. No one is out in the open."

"But…"

Through the pain, Christie summoned all his energy. "Go!"

Jack looked around. Angus and Sophie, oblivious to Jack's conversation with his dad, had finished tying up each of the soldiers, who were battered, but alive. Jack ran over, picked up the backpack and took out the explosive charge and detonator.

He called over to Sophie. "Sophie – I know you can drive a Kübelwagen – but can you manage that thing?" he gestured over to the motorbike and sidecar that still sat outside the entrance, its engine idling.

Sophie looked at him oddly, "No problem. Why?"

"Angus – you stay here and make sure those guys don't move. Try and patch Dad up... we'll be back... I hope."

"What are...?"

"No time to explain. Come on Sophie."

In a few seconds Sophie was straddling the Zündapp KS 750 and Jack hunkered down in the sidecar. Sophie revved the engine and looked down at Jack.

"Where to?"

"Follow the track that way, through the woods, it should take us straight to the launch pad."

The rear tyre spat up a plume of dust as Sophie threw the Zündapp into a tight turn and powered across the clearing to where the track curved into the woodlands. She redlined each gear in turn as they roared down the track. "How far?" she shouted to Jack, who clung on for dear life in the sidecar beside her.

"Quarter of a mile at most."

"What happens when we get there?"

"Get close to the silo – it will be obvious – in the middle of the next clearing. I'll set the charge and throw it into the silo on top of the rocket... should give us a few minutes to escape..."

At that moment, dead ahead, the track opened up into a small clearing. There was a flat concrete apron in the middle, and a circular, banked mound rose from the concrete pad, about two metres above the ground at its highest point. Beyond the mound was a tall crane and to the left was a large mechanical device that held a circular disc that had been lifted off the top of the mound like a giant lid. The narrow-gauge railway, built into the track, extended all the way to the mound. Parked up along the track were some army vehicles and what looked like three fuel tankers. Off to the right of the clearing, set far back from the concrete pad, where the clearing met the surrounding woodland, there was a strange-looking armoured vehicle with caterpillar tracks – a sort of stunted tank. Given all the vehicles and engineering equipment, Jack thought it strange that he could not see one person in the open. Suddenly, he understood why.

As they raced towards the mound, a plume of vapour exploded into the air directly ahead. They were only fifty metres away.

"Keep going – get as close as you can!" Jack yelled.

Sophie bent over the handlebars and twisted the throttle grip as the bike surged forward. Jack took the detonator and pushed it into the explosive. He set the timer. Ten seconds.

Then, amongst the gas and vapour spewing up from the mound there appeared a huge, black, pointed cone rising into the air. It was the rocket. It seemed to rise slowly at first, its twenty-five tons of thrust driven by the controlled explosion of the alcohol and oxygen, deep in its belly, fighting hard against the pull of gravity. In only twenty-four seconds the mighty projectile, with its lethal payload, would reach the speed of sound. In thirty-five seconds it would reach twice the speed of sound and in under a minute it would be twenty miles high, above the earth's atmosphere and travelling at more than five times the speed of sound. Minutes later it would arrive without warning above Portsmouth and detonate its deadly radioactive cargo, killing thousands of people and rendering the city uninhabitable.

The vast rocket loomed before them. Sophie had no time to

turn the bike away. It hit the mound and they were thrown upwards towards the rising rocket and the hot exhaust gases spewing up from the silo. Sophie twisted the handlebars to avoid smacking straight into the rocket and the whole bike lurched sideways. As the sidecar flashed past the rocket, Jack took the charge in one hand, reached out and slammed it onto the smooth, metal skin of the rocket. The adhesive clamped the explosive firmly to the V-2. The sidecar flew down the other side of the mound and slammed back onto the concrete apron. Jack and Sophie were thrown forward but managed to stay on the bike as it raced on towards the fencing at the far end of the launch pad. Sophie hit the brakes and wheeled the sidecar round. For a moment they gazed upwards as the mighty rocket cleared the silo.

"Don't wait!" Jack bellowed. "It's going to go off."

Sophie gunned the engine and they recrossed the launch pad, skirting past the silo and heading back down the access track towards the assembly houses and storage cave.

"Faster!" Jack shouted.

They had only travelled two hundred metres back down the track when the charge on the side of the rocket went off, immediately igniting the alcohol and oxygen tanks inside the rocket, directly above the launch pad. There was a white flash and the shockwave from the airburst caught them and propelled them down the track. Jack looked behind him as fire rained down from the heavens. It was as if half of France had gone up. No one underneath could possibly have survived. Then something else struck him. They had narrowly avoided the blast from the exploding fuel tanks... but they were as good as

V–2 rocket launch

dead anyway. The compartment with its radioactive payload would have surely fractured and would already be casting its invisible deadly radioactive dust across the French countryside. They had been irradiated and soon they would be dead. Just like Pendelshape.

Sophie brought the sidecar to a sudden halt. In the clearing next to the assembly houses, Tom Christie stood before them, supported by Angus. Jack jumped out of the sidecar and rushed towards his dad.

"It blew up… right above the launch pad… but the radioactive dust… we're all as good as dead…"

Christie clung on to his son, he wanted to comfort him, but he could find no words. He looked into his eyes and said, finally, "I'm sorry Jack." He took Sophie and then Angus by the hand, and said, "I'm so sorry…"

At first, they didn't notice the strange stunted tanklike vehicle that crawled its way towards them into the clearing from the access track. It moved slowly on caterpillar tracks and although it was clad in heavy armour, seemed to have no discernible guns or weaponry attached to it. The vehicle rumbled forward. One by one they turned to face it. It stopped about ten metres away from them. In the distance, they could see the plume of smoke rising from the woods where fires had been started by the burning remnant of the V-2. The four of them stood in a line staring at the vehicle. Christie could only stand supported by Angus. Jack and Sophie had scalding on their faces and hands from their close encounter with the rocket. They were all filthy, dishevelled and exhausted, and – knowing they were as good as dead – they no longer had the energy to fight or run.

Suddenly, a metal hatch on the roof of the tank clanged open and a man climbed out and stood up on top of the vehicle. At his throat he wore a black iron cross. He had a thin, scarred face and penetrating green eyes. At the centre of his cap there was an unusual silver emblem – a skull and crossbones. The Death's Head. Secreted in the armoured V-2 launch control vehicle, Axel Gottschalk had survived the destruction of the V-2 and now he pointed a machine gun down at them.

"Let me guess. British Intelligence," he shouted to Christie.

"It's over Gottschalk… we're all dead anyway."

"Over? It has only just begun. We have the plans… how long do you think it will take us to build another rocket; another bomb?" Gottschalk mocked.

"You are completely barking," Christie said, under his breath.

He shouted up to Gottschalk, "Perhaps you may be interested to know that Pendelshape had already passed us his plans." He was lying, but it was worth a final throw of the dice. "Yes… that's right. We've handed the plans on to the British military. And the RAF know all about this site and your research centre in Germany. Whatever you throw at them, you're going to get it right back with interest." Just for a moment, a look of doubt ghosted across Gottschalk's face. Then he reddened with pure rage and raised his weapon to fire.

But he never pulled the trigger.

From the woods off to their left there came a loud popping sound and something fizzed like a firework across the clearing towards the launch vehicle. It smacked plumb into the side of the vehicle and there was an ear-splitting explosion. As the smoke cleared, they could see that the launch vehicle was a wreck. The blackened body of Axel Gottschalk lay on the ground.

They turned towards the woods and watched as a figure emerged. He wore civilian clothes and a long, tubular device hung from one arm. Jack recognised the figure and as he got closer, his father limped forward to greet him.

"Albrecht. You survived!"

"Not just me," Altenberg said, smiling. "I have made some new friends…"

At that point Marianne and Jean-Yves ran towards them from the woods. Sophie's parents were alive. Pierre and Dominic followed behind. Sophie bolted forward and soon she was in her mother's arms, crying with joy.

"But how did you…?"

Altenberg smiled. "A bit of confusion during the accelerated countdown. But I still managed to swap the payload. Things did not happen quite as I planned them, but anyway, the radioactive material is safely on its way back to my laboratory at the Kaiser Wilhelm Institute in Berlin. From there I shall arrange a suitable resting place for it, just as we planned, Tom."

"So – we're not going to die?" Angus said.

Altenberg looked at him, "You look a bit the worse for wear, my friend, but I assure you, you do not have any radioactive poisoning…"

"But how did you rescue the others?"

Altenberg grinned. "I didn't. They were perfectly capable

of escaping on their own. What did you call it, monsieur?"

"Les jeux abnormales," Jean-Yves smiled.

"It was yesterday; they put us together – they were transferring us somewhere – the airport we think," Marianne said. "There was me, Jean-Yves, Pierre and Dominic. They killed all the others. We decided to take a risk. They didn't stand a chance. We then started searching for you three. Last night we hid out in the woods and this morning we discovered this place…"

"But you must go now, all of you," Altenberg said, urgently. "Soon the whole German army will be here. You must be well away before they arrive. They will be asking many questions."

"But what about you, Albrecht?" Christie said.

Altenberg shrugged. "We will blame this failure on another raid from the resistance Network. I will return to Germany and continue my work. For peaceful ends. You have helped me Tom. I now understand what I must do. I will pretend to help the Nazi war effort but I will, of course, ensure they are unable to develop radioactive materials. The reactor we built will be quietly dismantled. The plans will turn out to be deeply flawed. A British trick to waste our resources. We will cover up, blame it on Gottschalk, say that the weapon was not nearly ready. We will say that Gottschalk was too ambitious, too desperate to make an impact and imply that he had ambitions for the leadership of the Reich itself and that he had threatened all of us to keep us in line." He sighed, "I suspect that elements of the programme may continue – there were too many people involved with the rocket development, in particular. But the one thing I can ensure is that these rockets will never have nuclear materials on board. I hope, one day, some good will come of all this."

"And what about Petersen...?" Christie asked.

Altenberg gave another little shrug. "Like your colleague Pendelshape, Gottschalk had no further need for him. A sad business, I'm afraid."

Christie reached out and shook Altenberg's hand. "It was good working with you Albrecht – I hope you are right and that good might come of this... You never know – one day a rocket might take a man to the moon."

Altenberg laughed, "Now, Tom, you are just talking nonsense," he paused. "And what about the British? They have this technology of course... I suppose that means that one day it might be used against us – in Germany."

"The British government are not convinced. They are distracted and do not think they have the resources... they think it is just another mad scientist's dream..." Christie was lying. The British government, of course, knew nothing. But then Christie added, mischievously, "But maybe the Americans might be persuaded, one day."

"I can't see why, Tom," Altenberg replied. "Why on earth would the Americans want to join in another war in Europe? They would be mad."

"Are you two going to stop talking, because I think we need to go. I can hear voices coming down the track," Angus said nervously.

"Yes Angus – you're right. Albrecht, there are charges on the assembly houses. They are timed to go off later. You will need to deal with them. Now, we must go," Christie said.

"There are also some guards in the storeroom. I have secured them, but they are wounded. They'll need medical help."

"Thank you, Angus," Albrecht smiled. "We will blame you and your friends in the Network, of course. Pierre, take my weapon… they mustn't find me with it."

They quickly shook hands and headed back into the cave system. A few minutes later, some dazed soldiers emerged from the access track, guns at the ready. Altenberg had climbed up on the launch control vehicle, pretending to tend to Gottschalk. He pointed in the direction of the woods, away from the cave.

"A raid… a small group… that way, they went that way, hurry! One of you – come here and help me with the *Brigadeführer*. They got him – I think he is dead."

Altenburg knelt beside Gottschalk's corpse. The soldier leaned across to look at him.

"No hope. A tragic loss," Altenberg said.

He padded Gottschalk's charred uniform. As he did so, he felt a lump inside, just behind the breast pocket. Altenberg reached in and pulled something out. It was a piece of wood. He held it up to the light.

"What is it, Herr Altenberg?" the soldier said.

"Most strange. It seems to be a little toy boat. Look – it has a name – SMS *König*. How very odd. I wonder why it was in the *Brigadeführer's* pocket."

As they made their way back up through the cave system, Jack turned and whispered to his father, "Will he be OK? Altenberg I mean."

"Yes. From what I know of history he plays his cards brilliantly, no one will ever really know whether he was a Nazi supporter or if he deliberately prevented the development of a Nazi nuclear bomb… or whether he was just incompetent."

"He's not stupid is he?" Jack looked up. "And neither are you, are you, Dad?"

Christie put an arm round his son. "Runs in the family, Jack. I'm afraid it's got us into a bit of trouble now and again… but then, it's got us out of trouble as well."

Paris Adieu

It was three days since the destruction of the rocket at Villiers. They had made a clean getaway back through the limestone caves and a day later they were back in Paris where they holed up in a small, innocuous apartment in the Marais. Sophie, Marianne and Jean-Yves had left for the south soon after they had arrived back in Paris. Pierre and Dominic would also have to start a new life. It was too dangerous for them to stay. The farewell had been short but emotional. Sophie had hugged each of them and she'd had a tear in her eye as she said goodbye to Jack. Christie had repeated the instructions that he had given to them before: they should break all contact with the remnants of the Network and never speak to them, or of the events in which they had been involved in June 1940. Christie had explained that this was a matter of 'allied security' and above all it was for their own safety. But Jack and Angus knew otherwise. The family were sentenced to a quiet life. It was something, Jack felt, that all three of them – Sophie, Marianne and Jean-Yves – would probably find difficult.

With regular food and rest, Jack, Angus and Tom were on the mend. Jack had relished spending time with his dad and felt he understood him better now. He had finally told him what he'd seen as he and Angus had set off in the Taurus for 1940. But they all knew their adventure wasn't over and a sense of foreboding still hung in the air. They sat round the kitchen table in the apartment eating croissants and drinking coffee and pored over a large map that Christie had unfurled in front of them. This time the map was not of central Paris or of the area around Villiers-sur-Oise. It was a modern map, of somewhere much closer to home. They had already been through the plan ten times, but Jack had come to realise that his father was nothing if not thorough.

"So Jack, you said you entered the VIGIL site there," he pointed at a spot on the plan, "Entrance Two, is that right?"

"Yes – and I think it leads through that tunnel there to the Inner Hub, and then on to the Taurus Control Centre... there," Jack said.

Christie stared at the plans, pondering. "Yes – I remember it well."

"You remember it?" Angus exclaimed.

Christie smiled. "You're forgetting, Angus, I designed most of it. When I left, I took copies of all the plans, everything... my life's work... but never mind about that right now." He turned back to the map. "You say you were in the Control Centre when Belstaff and Johnstone jumped you and then you escaped in the Taurus, leaving the others behind?"

"Yes."

"Do you recall anything... anything at all: comments or images on the CCTVs about where the other Revisionist intruders were located on the site?"

"Yes – I think so," Jack said, pointing at two spots on the plan. "Here and here... I got the impression there were about six of them. And there were the others who attacked us up at Rachan."

Christie rubbed his chin, thoughtfully. "Interesting, that would explain why there were only a couple at the Revisionist base when I went there."

"Your team," Angus clarified. "Your ex-team, you know, the Revisionists – there weren't very many of you, then?"

"Not many – Pendelshape and a few others. Plus myself, before we had our little disagreement. But that's all we needed to run things. They managed to turn Belstaff and Johnstone, though – without them on the inside, of course, there is no way they could have mounted an all-out attack on VIGIL."

Christie sipped his coffee. "So I think we are ready then. We'll enter the site in exactly the same way and follow your route into the heart of the complex. I have an entry device and copies of all the security protocols, so it should be straightforward. When we get inside, we spring a little surprise for our friends Belstaff and Johnstone. Once we have control of the centre we can bring up the security systems and start to mop up the other intruders. No one knows their way round the systems in that place better than I do."

"So we just wait?"

Christie reached beneath his jacket and pulled out his time phone, placing it in the middle of the table on top of the map. Now they were safely in Paris, he had taken back Pendelshape's time phone from Jack, for safe-keeping.

"I have set the Revisionist Taurus to power up automatically every time there is a time signal."

He glanced over at equipment and weapons lying on the other side of the room. "We need to double-check that lot…"

"Dad, there is one thing I don't understand. VIGIL training says that you can't travel back to the point before you left… so how can you and I travel back, you know, before Angus and I escape to 1940?"

Christie smiled. "Good question, Jack. But we'll be using the *Revisionist* Taurus and my *Revisionist* time phone. From what you told me, I am pretty sure I followed Pendelshape back to 1940 *before* you escaped. Pendelshape should have waited till he was absolutely sure that VIGIL was under control. He made a mistake – went too early. He was always impatient. It was only an hour or so difference, but that's all we need. We'll be arriving back after I left. Two time machines – it makes the world a complicated and dangerous place. It was never meant to be like that."

Christie moved over for a final check of everything, including the weapons he had sourced in Paris.

"I hope it doesn't come to it… but we need to be prepared to use these…"

"We're ready, Tom," Angus said.

"Dad," Jack said. "The time phone… Look."

Christie hurried back over to the table. The small light was flashing. He opened it and inside the yellow bar winked back at them.

"OK, time to load up and gather round."

Christie checked the settings.

He looked up. "Everyone ready?"

Jack and Angus nodded.

"Gather round, touch the time phone and say *adieu* to Paris."

Gone

"**W**ell I have to say, Dad, you drive that thing far better than we do."

The time phone had landed them on the road next to the woods just outside the Soonhope High School estate.

"Keep your voice down," Christie whispered.

"There's the bike," Jack said. He pointed to where Angus and Jack had left the KTM. They crept forward.

"Engine's still hot…" Angus said.

"We can only be a few minutes, er, behind ourselves…" Jack said the words and immediately felt confused. "I'm still not used to this…"

"We must be extremely careful. Is this where you went inside?"

"Yes. Entrance Two is up through there."

They cut into the woods and after a short distance Christie stopped in his tracks. "This is it."

He reached inside his pocket and pulled out a control device. He pressed a button on the device and a small area in the undergrowth suddenly cleared, showing the circular metal covering set in a concrete base.

"Security systems are down. It will be easier than I thought. Step back." He pressed the device and the metal cover formed an aperture in the ground revealing a steep spiral staircase that lead downwards. One by one, they stepped onto the spiral staircase.

The stairs began to descend automatically. As they dropped beneath ground level, the aperture above them closed. Ahead of them was a door. Christie pressed the device again and it opened onto the short metal-clad corridor. At the end of the corridor was the circular door with five letters etched on it:

V I G I L

The door opened without a sound, revealing the tubular passageway beyond. It also revealed something else, something unexpected. Standing in the middle of the passageway was a slim woman. She was about forty and had grey-blue eyes and blonde hair. In her right hand she held an automatic pistol, which she held out at eye level, the butt cradled in her left palm. As the door swung open her eyes widened in astonishment and she slowly brought down the weapon.

"Mum?"

"Jack?" Carole Christie said incredulously. She ran over to her son and hugged him. "I thought they'd got you..."

She turned to her husband, "Tom... but how?"

Christie smiled. "It's nice to see you Carole... been a while. I see you got my message then? A close call."

Tom reached out and touched his wife on the cheek with his hand. She reached up and put her hand over his, holding it there for a few seconds.

"What's going on Tom? I only just got your warning. I decided to come straight here. I know I shouldn't but I was worried about Jack. Then I discovered there had been a security breach.

It's unbelievable. How did you get here so quickly…?"

"It's a long story, Carole. We've been on a bit of an adventure back in 1940. Don't have time to explain now – there are Revisionist intruders here. We need to stop them."

"It's happened again, hasn't it Tom? Why? What you've done… it's put Jack… me… in an impossible position… we're like playthings – stuck between you and Inchquin… you've nearly got us killed."

Christie shook his head. "I know, Carole, I know. I'm sorry… I thought I could manage it… but I couldn't… it all got out of control and then Pendelshape… I couldn't stop them… and now…"

"Tom, if we get through this…" she raised her voice, "it's got to stop. This stupid war between the Revisionists and VIGIL… we have to end it once and for all."

"We will Carole, we will. But right now we've got work to do. And we need your help."

For the first time in eight years Jack's mother and father were together. It should have been a happy moment for them, Jack thought, but they were bickering already.

"I want you and Angus to go up to Level Two – we think there are six Revisionist intruders up there. Jack and I are going to the Inner Hub. We should be able to take Belstaff and Johnstone by surprise and then bring up the security systems. That should allow us to lock down the intruders and then we can bring them in. OK?"

"OK," replied Carole.

They started to make their way along the passage. At each doorway they followed the same procedure – crouching low, guns at the ready as it swung open.

"OK, this is the Inner Hub access point. Angus, Carole – you can take the side door here up to Level Two. Be careful and wait until we have the systems back. I'll give you the signal."

Angus and Carole crept out of the side door and Christie looked at his watch. "Right Jack, we're two minutes from when you used the Taurus to escape to 1940. When I open this door there is another short passageway and at the end is the entrance to the Taurus Control Centre. If we have timed this correctly, it will be open and Johnstone and Belstaff will be busy trying to stop you and Angus escaping. You said that Gordon is hurt on the floor, that Inchquin, the Rector, Tony, Joplin and Turinelli will all be in there and Johnstone has been thrown back from the Taurus. We need to rush Belstaff. I'll take him out; you cover me and keep an eye on Johnstone. As soon as I open this door we go. Got it?"

Jack felt the adrenaline pumping through his veins. The image in his head of his view from the Taurus looking down at himself and his dad was clearer than ever. This moment had given him hope that had helped keep him alive; and now it had finally arrived. The only trouble was he didn't know what happened next.

Christie pushed through the door in front of them. As predicted, the entrance to the Control Centre was open.

"Go!" Christie shouted.

They rushed down the passageway and burst in to the Control Centre, arriving just as Johnstone was flying backwards through the air from the Taurus gantry, where he had reached into the Transfer Chamber. He landed awkwardly on the floor of the Control Centre. Belstaff had his back turned to them and was pointing his gun up at the Taurus platform. Jack saw himself and

Angus up on the transfer platform and, just for a split second, Jack caught his own eyes before he vanished through the temporary wormhole back to 1940.

"Drop it." Christie moved forward and pressed his gun into the back of Belstaff's neck. Belstaff froze and his weapon clattered to the floor. "On your knees." Belstaff dropped to the ground and Christie snatched up his weapon.

"Get something to tie these two up – though I don't think Johnstone is going to cause us too much trouble." Tony was quick to follow Christie's instruction. "Joplin – let me free you – then come over here and give me access to that terminal – we can bring the security systems back up."

Jack looked on at the astonished reactions of everyone in the room.

Inchquin was the first to speak, "But Tom... how on earth...?"

Christie did not look up as he pummelled the keyboard. "I thought I'd better come and help you guys out," he looked up briefly, "although if it weren't for Carole, Jack and Angus... I might not have bothered."

"Tom..." Inchquin started to speak.

"There..." Christie said, looking up at the screen with satisfaction. Security systems are back up. Joplin, you can now isolate each sector in turn as you see fit. Let's see – yes – there are intruders there and... there. Carole and Angus are up on Level Two, so you can instruct them to bring the intruders in once they know they can't escape and have put down their weapons. Tony can help bring in the others. You'll also need to deal with any of them outside the VIGIL site. We'd better get some medical help for him." Christie nodded at Gordon on the floor.

"We're saved," the Rector said. "I don't know how to thank you, Tom."

Christie got up from the terminal. "As I said, I'm not doing it for you." He looked across at Tony. "Those two secured?"

"They're not going anywhere," Tony said.

In some pain, Gordon managed to haul himself up from the floor. "My vest saved me – but I'm pretty sure I've got some colourful bruises…"

"Good." Christie turned to Inchquin, "Looks like you owe me one. Joplin – when the dust has settled you might want to do some analysis – make sure there is nothing else you need to tidy up in 1940 – we had a pretty interesting time back there."

Joplin was already concentrating on the security systems and he held a hand up to his headset. "Message from Angus: he and Carole are both safe; upper levels secured, intruders secured. They're coming back down." He turned to them and grinned. "It's over."

Christie walked over to Jack. He held him by the shoulders as he looked into his eyes. "Jack – I'm afraid I need to go. It's not safe for me to stay here. I know this seems strange but I hope you understand. First, I'm going back to the Revisionist base to tie up some loose ends. Then, I don't know what I will do… I need time to think a few things through. I think everything will be OK now." He turned to Inchquin, "Don't worry, I'm laying low for a while."

Jack looked into his father's eyes. "Dad… please don't go, it's like Mum said, it's over, isn't it? The Revisionists are finished… it's time to move on…"

Christie looked at Inchquin and scowled. "There's just too much water under the bridge, Jack, I can't do it. Not yet, anyway, I'm sorry. But maybe one day. One day I will return. For sure."

"But Dad… please," Jack pleaded.

"Sorry Jack, I have to go." There was a tear in his eye. "You look after Mum, OK?" He smiled ruefully and then Professor Tom Christie took out his time phone. The yellow light was still burning brightly. He pushed a button. There was a sudden, incandescent flash of white light and then, he was gone.

Déjà Vu

Just one week later there was the knock on the front door at Jack's home in Cairnfield.

It wouldn't be fair to say that things had got back to normal; after all, what was 'normal' about VIGIL and their lives now? Jack should have felt elated about their escape and the defeat of the Revisionists, but actually he felt he was in a state of limbo. Things which should have been sorted out had not been. Pendelshape was dead and the Revisionists had been destroyed and it even seemed possible that his dad would be reconciled with his old colleagues, Inchquin, the Rector and the rest of the VIGIL team. Jack had seen a moment of tenderness between his mum and dad – and he had hoped against hope that they would get back together. It had all been tantalisingly close to reconciliation and peace and then, at the final moment, his dad had decided that it was all too much of a leap of faith and that he would go and come back, 'maybe one day…' His dad's words went round and round in Jack's head and the more he thought about them, and what he and Angus had been through, the more frustrated he became.

He stared at Facebook on the big downstairs computer and occasionally fiddled with his new iPhone. That was one good thing: VIGIL had given him a replacement for the one he had lobbed into the Seine. But he couldn't be bothered with it all.

There was some outside summer party up river that evening... he and Angus were supposed to go, but Jack didn't feel like it. It all seemed a bit pointless and trivial after what they had been through. Sure, he got on with the other people his age in Soonhope, but sometimes the stress of keeping things secret was too much. At least there was Angus, but he seemed less bothered about everything than Jack; disappointed, almost, that they wouldn't be time travellers again, now the Revisionists were out of the way. VIGIL still had to be on their guard, of course. His dad was still at large – he had said he planned to return to the Revisionist base to think a few things through. Jack had no idea what he would do after that. They would just have to wait.

VIGIL had been busy tying up a few loose ends. There was the endless scrutiny of everything that had happened in 1940 and the historical variation analysis. Then there was the small matter of what to do with the Revisionist fugitives that had been caught inside VIGIL and the traitors, Johnstone and Belstaff. The men who had attacked Jack and Angus had finally been hunted down on the hills above the Grey Mare's Tail. There had been others who had been involved in raids on VIGIL personnel around Soonhope. They had all been caught now. Jack had no idea what VIGIL's procedures were in these circumstances. But he knew that they would be pumped for information and the secret whereabouts of the Revisionist base would soon be discovered. His father would not have long before he would have to say goodbye to it once and for all and move on again.

Then there had been the more trivial concern of trying to mend the window at Angus's place before his mum and dad had got back from their trip to the 'Sound of Music' – not to mention plastering over two bullet holes in the kitchen wall. Angus had reported that his parents had noticed nothing, although his dad was furious that Angus had come off the KTM XC 450 and scraped it all down one side. He had no idea, of course, how the damage had really been done and that, but for Angus's superb driving skills, the bike would have been a write-off and he would have been attending Angus and Jack's funerals.

There was also the problem of recovering a time phone from the top of Nelson's column. It was an operation not without risk and if anyone was around at the other end when a time-traveller arrived, it would give them a bit of a surprise. All these things Jack was more than happy to leave to VIGIL to worry about. And from VIGIL's perspective, once again, Jack and Angus had proved their worth. This time Angus had high expectations of a reward and he had already brazenly expressed his wish for something better than a new iPhone.

Again, the knock at the front door. This time harder. Jack remembered – Mum was out. He didn't rush to answer it.

There was a woman standing on the doorstep. She looked up at him. Jack was a little taken aback. She was very old and quite frail – certainly in her eighties. She had grey hair and dark, weather-beaten skin and behind her glasses Jack could see that her eyes were brown.

"Hello," Jack said.

The old woman looked at him oddly. She seemed quite surprised by something.

"I'm, er, sorry, but I was looking for someone. I believe this is the Christie household. Is your father in…? Or your grandparents, perhaps?"

The question seemed a little strange and the old woman continued to stare at Jack in a rather disconcerting manner, almost as though she recognised him. But Jack was sure he'd never seen her before in his life.

"Well… my father is away, but Mum is in town. She'll probably be back soon."

"And the rest of your family, grandparents… er, grandfather?"

"I'm afraid they died some years ago, they did live here though. Did you know them?"

The woman suddenly looked rather sad.

"I'm sorry – would you like to come in – maybe sit down? Some tea perhaps?"

"Tea? How English. That would be very kind. I am a little tired."

The woman's English was excellent but now Jack picked up a slight accent.

"Come in. So it is my grandparents you were looking for? Come through, the kitchen is just in here…"

They went into the kitchen and Jack put on the kettle.

"You can sit down there if you like."

Jack pulled out a chair. Suddenly, the woman clasped his wrist and brought her face close to Jack's as though she was searching for something. It was a little alarming.

"It's uncanny my dear, quite uncanny."

"Er, sorry, what is?"

"You! You're the spitting image of him. Same hair, same face, same voice: the spitting image. And your name is Jack, isn't it dear?"

"Yes – how did you…?"

"The same name too," the old woman smiled. "It is extraordinary."

Jack eased his wrist free. "Sorry – who am I like?"

"Your grandfather, of course. Well I assume he was your grandfather. Sit down, dear, let me show you something. I was never supposed to speak of it, but now, well, I'm old and it was many years ago, so what harm could come of it?"

The woman had a handbag which she put on the table. She pulled out a slim, well-worn leather folder. It looked almost as old as she did. "I kept most of them, even though I knew it might be dangerous. Why don't you take a look?" The old woman nodded at the folder lying unopened on the table in front of them.

Jack opened it. Inside there were a number of old black-and-white photographs. He looked at them closely, and, with growing astonishment, he started to understand.

The first photograph was of the Eiffel Tower, taken from some distance away. The top of the tower was in low cloud. The tail fin of an aeroplane was sticking out of the tower just below the cloud line. The photo was exactly the same as the one that Angus's dad had shown them at Rachan. The old woman smiled.

"And that one…"

The second photograph was of Jack and Angus. They were on a narrow platform way up in the air, surrounded by metal girders. They both seemed beaten up and Angus was covered in blood. He looked up into the old woman's eyes and they transported him back seventy years to wartime Paris, as he recognised her at last: Sophie. Jack was stunned.

"There," she pointed. "That's your grandfather – Jack was his name – the same as yours. He was a pilot in the RAF and that is his friend, Angus. What an adventure we had! I was not supposed to speak of it and it has been my secret for many, many years. Although the photo of the Eiffel Tower and the Spitfire, I admit, I sold when we went through hard times after the war…"

Questions crowded into Jack's head… "What happened to you… after the war? How come you are here?"

"We were in the resistance you know. But in 1940 we escaped Paris and went south. Mother and Father tried to live a quiet life. British Intelligence ordered it. We ended up in Grenoble and they died there, peacefully, many years ago. I set up a photographic studio… and later we had a shop – climbing, skiing, Parkour. My father had a special name for it, he called it 'les jeux abnormales'. She smiled and her whole face wrinkled. "We had a good life and good fun… eventually. But…" she shrugged, "I never forgot your grandfather… and I hoped one day we would meet again. I did try and make contact, after the war. But I could find nothing, nothing at all. It was as if he had vanished off the face of the earth. I have my own family now… five grandchildren! But still I have kept looking, kept hoping.

One day I was doing some research into my photograph. It became quite famous you know – the one of the Spitfire in the Eiffel Tower. It was always a mystery who the pilot was, and I never told anyone. I learned more about the story behind it. About the Northolt Raid and the Battle of Britain. I heard about a Hurricane pilot – a man called Ludwig Jud – who had been involved in the Raid. I followed the trail and then I discovered that his descendants still lived in Scotland. A place called Rachan, near here. And that's why I decided to come here."

"You've been to Rachan?" Jack said, increasingly anxious.

"My family thought I was stupid to travel all this way at my age. But I was insistent. I am staying in Edinburgh and I went and paid the Jud family a little visit yesterday. Do you know that Ludwig Jud's grandson still farms up there? Of course, he knows the story about his grandfather Ludwig very well. We had a wonderful chat. It's unbelievable, but he is actually restoring the plane that crashed into the Eiffel Tower. He even had a copy of my photograph. It was a thrilling moment for me. We talked some more. The Juds were very kind and told me all about their friends and life in the Soonhope Valley and then, it was very strange, because they talked about their son. He wasn't there but he's called Angus – they're very proud of him. He's a good sportsman apparently. They showed me a picture of him with the rugby trophy. They talked about his friends and they mentioned the name of his best friend – a Jack – Jack Christie. That's you, Jack, isn't it? They told me that you lived just outside Soonhope. You had the same name as the Jack I knew and I thought, well, there might just be a chance that it's the same family – or at least the family might be related in some way to the Jack I knew. So I had to come and visit."

She looked deep into his eyes. "So Jack, does any of this make any sense? Do you know anything about your family history…? Was your grandfather in the war? Could he have been the pilot of the Spitfire? Could he have been my Jack? Or are there are other Christies that you have heard of? Do you know? Because no trace was ever found of him. If he survived the war and he had children, it has been the world's best-kept secret."

Jack was starting to sweat. He sensed Sophie's turmoil. She had been searching all her life, for him, for Jack. He desperately wanted to blurt out the truth and tell her everything. He tried to think of a way out.

"I'm sorry," he said. "I'm afraid our family, is a little dull… Nothing exciting like that has happened to any of us." He didn't sound very convincing.

"Oh, I see." Sophie gave him a doubtful look. "I thought it might be too much to hope for. He must have died later in the war or something. That's what I always thought… but there was no trace, you see. Nothing. I'm like a silly girl sometimes. I suppose I am still a bit in love with him even after all these years. So silly." She paused and looked at him intently, with a twinkle in her eye. "But, Jack, maybe you can help me anyway?"

"Of course. I'll try."

"I think I will die soon. If I ever found my Jack, well, I wanted to make sure I said 'goodbye'. Properly I mean. You look just like him and sound just like him and even have the same name, so we could *pretend*, couldn't we?"

"Sorry?"

"We could *pretend* that you are him and I can give these to you, my photographs. If you accept them…" she put a wrinkled hand over his and squeezed it gently, "… you will make an old woman very happy."

Jack felt a lump in his throat. "Thank you, Sophie. I will look after them. It's an incredible story and you are an incredible person. I would love to keep them."

Suddenly, Sophie's demeanour changed. Her eyes narrowed. It was as if she were trying to work something out in her head. "You know some things about the time I spent with my Jack never made sense to me. He seemed to know things. And for some reason his father was there, working for British Intelligence. Jack didn't want me to find out, but when I did he swore me to secrecy. Seemed strange, on reflection. And it was odd, you know, but of course, Jack had a friend – the other pilot who flew the Spitfire. His name was Angus. Angus Jud. The son of the family I met at Rachan yesterday had exactly the same name. Very strange. Two men, Ludwig and Angus, with the same surname fighting in the same air battle I might think was possible. But two boys living in this valley with exactly the same names, seventy years later, who, well, look identical. It is most odd."

Jack looked at her anxiously.

"And Jack, I could not help but notice, that device on the table. I think it's called an iPhone, isn't it? I am not very good with modern things – but you can use it to play music… and I like music. You might be surprised, I like modern music."

Jack glanced at his iPhone nervously.

"And, I'm afraid I was very rude, when we met at the door. I didn't mention my name and yet, you already seemed to know it. You called me Sophie."

"But, I…"

She smiled, "So tell me, Jack, do you and your friend Angus

still listen to Arcade Fire on your iPhone? I'm eighty-five and I love them. In fact I was probably into them before you were."

Sophie looked at Jack mischievously. "I must say, I'm getting a little confused, so I'm hoping that perhaps you can help me understand all this. Am I confused? Is it my age? Or have you got something to tell me, Jack?" Her eyes twinkled. "Well – have you?"

Jack's lips curved into a smile. "I'm sorry Sophie, I didn't want to say… it's kind of against all the rules. But I think we can make an exception for you. I do have something to tell you. And you're not confused. I'd say you're as sharp as a tack. You might want to have that cup of tea now. In fact, you might need something a bit stronger. Mum has some French brandy somewhere – I think it's called Bonaparte's."

The Taurus and Time Travel – Some Notes

The Taurus and its energy source always stay in one place. In order to move through time and space, the traveller needs to have physical contact with a time phone, which is controlled and tracked through a set of codes connected with the Taurus. Time travel is only possible, however, when the Taurus has enough energy and when there is a strong carrier signal. As Jack and Angus have discovered, the signal can be as unpredictable as the weather. The time signals are also highly variable – periods of time open up and then close, like shifting sands, so that no location is constantly accessible. Deep time is a specific constraint, which means that the traveller cannot visit a time period less than thirty years in the past. Anything more recent is a no-go zone. Finally, there is the 'Armageddon Scenario', which suggests that, if you revisit the same point of space–time more than once, you dramatically increase the risk of a continuum meltdown. Imagine space–time as a piece of tissue paper – each visit makes a hole in that tissue paper, as if you had pushed through the tissue with your finger. The tissue would hold together for a while, but with too many holes, it would disintegrate. It is dangerous, therefore, to repeat trips to the same point. The precise parameters of this constraint are not known and have not, of course, been tested.

TIMELINE OF THE SECOND WORLD WAR

1939

Hitler invades Poland

UK and France, known as the Allied forces, declare war on Germany

1941

Operation Barbarossa begins – the Nazi invasion of Russia

Japan bombs Pearl Harbor, USA

The USA declares war on Japan and joins the Allied forces

1944

D Day: The Allied invasion of France begins

Paris is liberated

Allies defeat Germans at the Battle of the Bulge

Russians reach Berlin

1940

Churchill becomes Prime Minister of Britain

Denmark, Norway, Luxembourg, Netherlands and Belgium surrender to German 'Blitzkrieg' or 'lightning war'

British and French troops evacuated to Great Britain at Dunkirk, France

France surrenders to the Nazis and the Vichy government is formed

Battle of Britain begins. German Luftwaffe bombs British RAF air bases

The Blitz begins – British cities bombed by Nazis

Germany, Japan, and Italy, known as the Axis powers, sign a military alliance called the Tripartite Pact

British victory in Battle of Britain. Hitler is forced to postpone plans to invade

1942

American naval victory against Japan at Battle of Midway in the Pacific Ocean

At Auschwitz, the mass murder of Jewish people begins

1943

German troops suffer major defeat at Stalingrad in Russia

Allied victory in North Africa

Allied victory at the Battle of the Bismarck Sea against Japanese troops

Italy signs secret armistice with Allies

1945

Hitler commits suicide and Germany surrenders

After the USA drops atomic bombs on Hiroshima and Nagasaki, Japan surrenders

MAP OF EUROPE DURING THE SECOND WORLD WAR

Unable to make progress in the west after defeat at the Battle of Britain, Hitler began an invasion of Russia to the east in 1941. By 1945, Allied troops had triumphed and Germany surrendered, ending the biggest conflict in history.

Day of Vengeance

 BACKGROUND INFORMATION

In Day of Vengeance, Jack and Angus travel back to Britain and France in 1940, just after the defeat of France and the evacuation from Dunkirk, during the early part of the Second World War. This was a momentous period in world history and one where Hitler's 'Third Reich' was approaching the peak of its powers. The notes below give a little more information on the events and people of the time.

What was the Second World War?
The Second World War started in 1939 and ended in 1945 with the defeat of Germany and Japan. It was the biggest and worst military conflict in human history, during which over fifty million people died. It extended to Europe, Northern Africa, the Soviet Union, the United States, the Middle East, the Far East and Japan. The war completely changed the balance of political and economic power in the world. *Day of Vengeance* focuses on only a short period at the start of the Second World War in 1940 – just after the defeat of France by Germany and just before the Battle of Britain. At this point, the Soviet Union, United States and Japan were not yet involved in the war.

What was the Battle for France? (see page 128)
On 10th May 1940, the Germans launched '*Blitzkrieg*' (Lightning War) in the west, invading the Netherlands, Belgium and France.

The Netherlands surrendered within six days. On 28th May, Belgium surrendered and, on 4th June, the bulk of British forces (allied with France) were successfully evacuated, along with remnants of the French army, from the northern French Channel port of Dunkirk. The German victory had taken less than seven weeks. France, a major European power with one of the largest armies in the world, had been defeated by the might of the German armed forces, known as the *Wehrmacht*, which included fast-moving tank divisions supported by armoured, mobile infantry and air support from fighters and dive bombers. On 22nd June, the French government signed an armistice with Germany. It was the most humiliating military disaster in French history. The defeat stunned the world and at that moment, Britain stood alone against the Nazis.

What was the Battle of Britain? (see page 35)

Following the defeat of France, the Germans intended to invade Britain using a plan called Operation Sea Lion. Some historians now think that Hitler was not seriously planning to invade – he was just hoping to force Britain to sign a peace treaty. In preparation for their invasion, the German air force (the *Luftwaffe*) launched air attacks on Britain that aimed to defeat the Royal Air Force to allow free passage for the naval invasion force. Britain was alone at this point, and some British politicians had lost hope. They thought that Britain should agree a peace settlement with the Nazis. Prime Minister Winston Churchill was determined that

Britain should fight on, alone or not. The Germans launched air attacks from their new bases in France and the Netherlands, but they were unable to break down the RAF. Then, in return for British planes bombing Berlin, Hitler changed tactics and began bombing British cities – this was devastating for many civilians, but it gave the RAF a short respite, which enabled them to rebuild their strength. Eventually, Hitler gave up on his plans to invade Britain and finally, in 1941, he turned his attention to the east – the invasion of the Soviet Union. He also declared war on the United States in December 1941, following the Japanese attack on Pearl Harbor.

The Battle of Britain kept Britain in the war, which later allowed the Allies to launch D-Day from Britain in order to reoccupy Western Europe. The 'Northolt Raid' (see page 31), described in *Day of Vengeance*, is fictitious, as is the description of the base and the aircraft located there (Northolt was a Hurricane base at this stage). However, raids did occur on RAF bases later on during the Battle of Britain.

Why were the RAF able to resist the Luftwaffe in the Battle of Britain?

Both sides were well-matched but the RAF had some advantages. They had radar, so they knew when the enemy aircraft were coming. With this information, the British fighter aircraft – Spitfires and Hurricanes – could be up in the air, waiting for the enemy. The RAF also had some great leaders who had insisted on investment before the war. A strong system of communication between the radar and lookout stations, central control and the airfields had been built in advance. The Germans had the disadvantage of fighting over enemy territory, so when their pilots bailed out they could be taken prisoner. The location also meant they had further to travel and the fighter planes had limited fuel. Then there was the German tactical error of switching from the assault on the RAF itself to bombing cities. The men on both sides were extremely brave and many died. However, in purely military terms, Britain's ability to resist was remarkably 'efficient' in terms of loss of life. Around 550 allied pilots died – very few casualties in comparison with some of the other murderous campaigns in the war – yet the pilots prevented German invasion and kept Britain fighting. At this point, ten European states had already fallen to German occupation, with grim results. Success in the Battle of Britain paved the way for eventual victory on the Western Front. On 20th August 1940, in a speech to inspire his country, Winston Churchill said, "Never in the field of human conflict was so much owed by so many to so few." Following this speech, the pilots and aircrew from many countries who fought for Britain became known as 'The Few'. They remain an inspiration to this day.

What was the Vengeance programme? (see page 36)

Towards the end of the war, German scientists developed flying bombs called V-1s. 'V' stands for Vengeance. The Germans also developed rockets carrying conventional explosive warheads called V-2s, which were launched from sites in Northern France onto London, Paris and the Netherlands. There were a number of other weapons in development, including a 'V-3' – a giant cannon. Construction of the V-3 was undertaken at the Pas de Calais, but was put out of use by the RAF before it was ever fired. During the later stages of the war, Germany was losing and Hitler was desperate to find a 'miracle weapon' that could redress the balance. However, the efforts drained money, expertise and manpower from the production of more conventional, but better tried and tested weapons. Although the V-1s and V-2s were frightening and could cause a lot of damage, not enough of them were produced to have much of an impact on the course of the war.

The holy grail of the Vengeance programme was to couple Germany's expertise in missile technology with a nuclear, chemical or biological weapon. However, their nuclear research did not advance quickly enough and was too fragmented to achieve this. In contrast, the Americans took a somewhat different approach during the war. They invested vast amounts of money and expertise in the Manhattan Project, which developed the nuclear weapons dropped on Japan in 1945 at Hiroshima and Nagasaki – but these were delivered 'conventionally' from a bomber aircraft, rather than by a missile.

In *Day of Vengeance*, the implication that in 1940 Germany had a working V-2 equipped with a nuclear 'dirty bomb' payload is fictitious. The first V-1 was launched against London on 13th June 1944. A total of 9,251 V-1s were fired at the United Kingdom, killing over 6,000 civilians and injuring nearly 18,000 people. The first V-2 was launched against London from the Hague, in the

Netherlands, on 8th September 1944. A total of 1,115 V-2s were fired at the United Kingdom killing nearly 3,000 civilians in London and injuring a further 6,500.

Did German scientists really work on the Apollo space programme? (see page 36)

Yes. After the war, many of the best German scientists were recruited by other countries to assist in weapons development programmes. When it was discovered that Nazi scientists were working on the American Apollo space programme it caused a scandal. This was known as the 'Paperclip Conspiracy', because clips were used to mark the files of German recruits.

What was the French Resistance?

The French Resistance is the name given to resistance movements that fought against the Nazi German occupation of France and against the Vichy regime – the collaborationist French government put in place by the Nazi regime. The Resistance conducted guerrilla warfare, published underground newspapers, provided intelligence to the Allies and helped Allied soldiers and airmen, trapped behind enemy lines, to escape. The French Resistance played a significant role in helping the Allies' advance through France, following the invasion of Normandy on 6th June 1944.

The *Croix de Lorraine* (see page 138) was chosen by General

Charles de Gaulle as the symbol of the Resistance. Charles de Gaulle became leader of the French government in exile and later on after the war, Prime Minister and then President of France. In *Day of Vengeance*, the implication that there was an organised French resistance as early as June 1940, that they planned to assassinate Hitler on his visit to Paris and that the *Croix de Lorraine* was its known symbol by that time, is fictitious.

Did the French really break the lifts on the Eiffel Tower? (see page 103)

Yes. They claimed that they did not have the right parts to fix it; but mysteriously, following the German surrender, the lifts were working again within hours.

In *Day of Vengeance*, the crash of the Spitfire into the Eiffel Tower is fictitious, additionally, getting two boys into the cockpit of a Spitfire is possible – but a very tight squeeze! There is an account of two adults piloting a Spitfire, strictly against regulations, on their way to a party in 1940. They never came back.

What is Parkour? (see page 104)

Parkour is a non-competitive 'sport', that began in France, in which people run along a route, negotiating obstacles using only their own bodies. This typically involves jumping, climbing and rolling and is often practised in urban areas. A practitioner of Parkour is called a *traceur* (male) or *traceuse* (female). Parkour is thought to originate from a system of physical education, developed by a French naval officer called Georges Hébert, which became part of the French system of military training during the world wars. Hébert was one of the proponents of *parcours*, which literally means 'route' (shortened from *parcours de combattant* – 'obstacle course'). There is debate as to whether Parkour is the same as *l'art du déplacement* or freerunning. In *l'art du déplacement* the practitioner seeks to move quickly and creatively past obstacles, whereas freerunning can be a competition sport, which includes the use of 'tricks', like rotations and spins. Parkour is about getting from one place to another as quickly and efficiently as possible. The depiction of Parkour in *Day of Vengeance* is fictional.

Who was Adolf Hitler?
Adolf Hitler (1889 to 1945) was an Austrian-born German politician and the leader of the National Socialist German Workers Party – better known as the Nazi Party. He was Chancellor of Germany from 1933 to 1945 and, after 1934, also head of state – as *Führer* (leader) – ruling Germany as a dictator. During this time he transformed Germany into a single-party dictatorship. Hitler wanted to reverse the outcome of the Treaty of Versailles, which ended the First World War, establish German dominance over continental Europe, reuniting all German people within the Reich, and to expand the Reich to the east to achieve '*Lebensraum*' ('living space') for his people. His aggressive strategy culminated in the invasion of Poland in 1939, which triggered the United Kingdom

and France to declare war against Germany, leading to the outbreak of the Second World War.

During this time, Hitler and the Nazis were responsible for the murder of millions of people. The 'Holocaust' – a programme to rid Germany and Europe of all elements considered by the Nazis to be 'unworthy of life' – saw the deaths of six million Jews, five million Russians, two million Poles, half a million gypsies and half a million other people.

In the final days of the war, during the Battle of Berlin in 1945, Hitler married his long-time mistress Eva Braun. The two committed suicide on 30th April 1945, less than two days later.

Who was Winston Churchill?

Winston Churchill (1874 to 1965) was Prime Minister of the United Kingdom during the Second World War from 1940 to 1945 (and again after the war from 1951 to 1955). He is regarded as one of the greatest wartime leaders of all time. He was also a historian, journalist and writer (winning the Nobel Prize for Literature) and an artist. Churchill was an officer in the British army and went on to hold many positions of authority during his career, including First Lord of the Admiralty, Secretary of State for War and Chancellor of the Exchequer. After the resignation of Neville Chamberlain, Churchill became Prime Minister of the United Kingdom and led Britain to victory. A great speaker, Churchill made wartime speeches that galvanised Britain and its supporters against the Nazis. In his speech on 4th June 1940, following the evacuation from Dunkirk, he said:

> *We shall not flag or fail. We shall go on to the end, we shall*
> *fight in France, we shall fight on the seas and oceans, we*
> *shall fight with growing confidence and growing strength in*
> *the air, we shall defend our island whatever the cost may*
> *be, we shall fight on the beaches, we shall fight on the*
> *landing grounds, we shall fight in the fields and in the*
> *streets, we shall fight in the hills; we shall never surrender…*

His state funeral was attended by one of the largest ever assemblies
of statesmen from around the world.

Was Albrecht Altenberg a real person? (see page 114)

Albrecht Altenberg is a fictional character, but there were a
number of physicists working in Germany at the time. The most
famous was Werner Heisenberg, who made significant
contributions to quantum mechanics and is best known for the
'uncertainty principle' of quantum theory. Heisenberg was
awarded the 1932 Nobel Prize in Physics. In 1939, after the
discovery of nuclear fission, the German nuclear energy project,
also known as the Uranium Club, was begun and Heisenberg was
engaged by the Nazis to support their research efforts.

In 1942, Heisenberg was summoned to report to Albert Speer,
Germany's Minister of Armaments (who also toured Paris with
Hitler in 1940), on the prospects for converting the Uranium
Club's research towards developing nuclear weapons. During the
meeting, Heisenberg told Speer that a nuclear bomb could not be
built before 1945. There remains controversy about Heisenberg's

involvement in the Nazi's nuclear programme, the level of his commitment and the extent of his political affiliations. There is also debate about why the programme had achieved relatively little by the end of the war. Although work continued on reactor design through the war, evidence shows that the Germans did not come close to building a working reactor that could be used to develop material for a nuclear weapon.

Did Hitler travel to Paris in 1940? (see page 119)

Yes. Hitler's only visit to Paris took place at 6 a.m. on 28th June 1940 and original footage of his visit exists today. Hitler's entourage stopped at a number of famous Paris landmarks: the Opéra, the Madeleine, the Eiffel Tower, Les Invalides and Sacré-Coeur. Albert Speer, Hitler's chief architect, and Brekel, a sculptor, accompanied Hitler on the tour.

What was the SS? (see page 111)

The SS – an abbreviation of *Schutzstaffel* or 'Protection Squadron' – was an 'army within an army' devised by Adolf Hitler and commanded by Heinrich Himmler. It was formed in 1925 as a personal guard unit for Adolf Hitler and grew from a small paramilitary group to become one of the most powerful organisations in Nazi Germany. The SS was responsible for some of the most shocking crimes of the Nazi era. In *Day of Vengeance*, SS officer Axel Gottschalk is a fictional character.

Acknowledgements

Many thanks to Sara Newbery (fellow Soonhopian) for her help on the French scenes, Alison and David Stubley, Ann and Roger South, Amanda Wood, Ruth Huddleston, Anne Finnis, Ruth Martin, Helen Greathead, Will Steele, Ian Butterworth, Tom Sanderson, Phil Perry, Jayne Roscoe, Victoria Henderson, Richard Scrivener, Jonny Lambert, Caroline Knox and Pam Royds. Thanks too, as ever, to Sally, Peter, Tom and Annie and friends and family who continue to support Jack and Angus on their escapades through history.

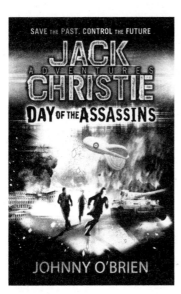

DAY OF DELIVERANCE

by Johnny O'Brien

In his second perilous mission, Jack travels back to an Elizabethan England riddled with treacherous plots. Amid sea battles, sword fights and subterfuge, Jack must defend the life of the queen, her kingdom, and the world as we know it. Dark dealings and deadly intrigue set the scene for the second thrilling journey in the Jack Christie Adventures.

Paperback £5.99
ISBN 978-1-84877-097-3

ePub ISBN 978-1-84877-107-9
Mobi ISBN 978-1-84877-115-4

www.jackchristieadventures.com